VADIR

STAR-CROSSED ALIEN MAIL ORDER BRIDES

SUSAN HAYES

ABOUT THE BOOK

What do you do when your planet runs out of women?
Send for takeout, of course.

Vadir has a business empire to run and no time to spare on frivolous endeavors. So how did he wind up on the far side of the galaxy to claim a mate he never signed up for? A m

His plan is simple: meet the female, negotiate terms, and leave the primitive planet of Earth as fast as he can. What could possibly go wrong?

This book contains a bohemian blonde with a hell of a right hook, and an interstellar tycoon who is about to learn that the best things in life can't be bought or sold, they have to be won.

SUSAN HAYES

ALL RIGHTS RESERVED: This literary work may not be reproduced or transmitted in any form or by any means, including electronic or photographic reproduction, in whole or in part, without express written permission.

All characters and events in this book are fictitious. Any resemblance to actual persons living or dead is strictly coincidental. It is fiction so facts and events may not be accurate except to the current world the book takes place in.

Copyright © 2017 Susan Hayes

Vadir (Book #2 of the Star-crossed Alien Mail Order Brides Series)

First E-book Publication: October 2017

Cover Design: crocodesigns.com

Editor: Dayna Hart

Published by: Black Scroll Publications

ISBN: 978-1-988446-21-9

DEDICATION

As always, this story is dedicated to my Mum and Dad, for their love and support of their sometimes crazy daughter.

This book is also dedicated to Karen, who is the 'sister of my heart,' and a dear friend no matter how many miles are between us.

1

____

Vadir Rahal paced the floor of his office and tried to think of a way out of this insane predicament. He didn't have time for this right now. What was the King thinking?

Turning his back on the sweeping view of the city outside his windows, he stormed back to his desk and snatched the thick piece of parchment off the surface.

No one used parchment anymore. It had been an outdated concept two hundred years ago, but the royal family loved their traditions. The damned thing had even been delivered by a royal messenger in full uniform. He read the words again, looking for a loophole. Something, anything that he could use to decline the *honour* bestowed on him by the King and Queen of Pyros.

There wasn't one.

"By the Flames of the First One, why did it have to be me?" he tossed the royal decree back onto the desktop and started pacing again.

"I've got a half-dozen deals to broker in the next week alone, and the Qualla Mining Consortium is threatening a work stoppage that could affect the ore markets for years to come. I need to be here, not on the other side of the galaxy retrieving my mate. I don't need a mate. I didn't ask for one. Crown Prince Joran is the one who needs a..."

He stopped in his tracks. Joran. If anyone could get him out of this, it would be the prince. He activated a wall monitor and called the one man on the planet who had any chance of changing the King's mind.

"So, I guess you got the decree?" Joran asked by way of greeting.

"You knew about this?"

The Prince nodded. "I'm going with you. Turns out, you're not the only one whose mate is supposedly on that planet."

"Why me? Is this because I refused to play nice with the Romakis during that last trade war? Is this your father's idea of revenge?"

"Wrong parent."

"Your *mother* did this to me? I thought she liked me!"

"She does. Which is why she insisted your profile be included when we screened for possible mates. The rest was luck, or if you believe my mother, the will of the Gods."

"So, this is real? My mate is out there?" The air in his perfectly maintained office suddenly seemed too thin.

"That's what the experts say. They may not be our true mates, but our scientists confirm we can have children with them."

"How can they possibly know that?"

Joran laughed. "I asked the same question. The answer is hard to believe, but I've seen the reports. Some of these people, humans, already carry Pyrosian genes."

"How?" Vadir demanded, too stunned by the revelation to manage more than a single word.

"I'll send you the report, and our experts' best guess as to how it happened. It makes for interesting reading, but the short version is, this is real."

"Our mates are out there, on another planet? And we're just going to wander over there, explain matters, and bring them back here? Do you know how insane that sounds?"

Joran nodded. "I know. Read the reports. You've got enough time to make whatever preparations are necessary, but you can't tell anyone where you're going. We'll figure out a cover story, probably something about you and I taking the *Firebrand* out on its maiden voyage to tour the system. Your shipyard built it, so no one will question why you're coming along."

"If you want it to be believable, I should bring my private shuttle, too. Everyone knows I have control issues."

Joran snickered. "Fine, I'll leave room in the hangar for your ship. But don't think I don't know what you're doing. If you want to fly yourself down to the planet, you're going to need to clear that with Commander Denza. He's in charge of the mission."

Of course he was. Who else would the King entrust with the life of his son and heir? "I'll talk to him. I may have to obey this decree, but I'm not going to negotiate mating terms with some alien female surrounded by royal guardsmen. There are advantages to being me."

"Just be on board and on time." Joran grinned at him. "I'm sure you can negotiate the rest of the details to your satisfaction."

"I wouldn't dream of being late. An order is an order." And apparently, this was one command he wasn't going to be able to charm or buy his way around. Vadir recalled the final line of the missive he'd received. *You will go to Earth and determine if the female is your mate. If she is, then you are hereby commanded to bring her home to Pyros.* "I don't suppose I'm going to be allowed to do some trade negotiations while I'm there?"

Joran laughed at him. "Father said you'd ask, and his answer is no."

"I had to try."

"Of course you did. We'll talk again soon. I'll send you over the file with all the information we have on your match. It's not much, but at least you can see what she looks like. Her name is Lisa."

Joran signed off, leaving Vadir alone in his office.

I'm going to be mated. The thought hit him with the force of a rogue comet strike. He'd never imagined this day would come. Hadn't planned on it. Why would he, when there were so few unmated females on Pyros? He enjoyed the occasional dalliance with females from the planets he visited for business, but those were simple, short-term affairs. Taking a mate was anything but simple, which was why Vadir had hoped to avoid it. But not even his wealth and power allowed him to refuse a royal command.

Faced with a new challenge, Vadir did what he did best. He set aside his emotions and focused on making a plan. He'd been ordered to negotiate the biggest deal of his life, and failure was not an option. If the King and Queen wished him to bring back a mate, then that's what he'd do.

He needed to know as much about this Lisa as he

could. Every being he'd ever met had a price. This female would be no exception. All he had to do was determine what she wanted, and offer it to her in exchange for leaving her primitive, isolated world to join him on Pyros and live in luxury for the rest of her life. It should be an easy sell.

———

Business had been slow all day, but that suited Lisa Woods just fine. She was still nursing a hangover from the wine she'd drunk last night. Or maybe it was an ice cream overdose. She pondered that idea for a moment and then rejected it. There was no such thing as too much ice cream.

There had definitely been too much wine, though. That's the only reason she had broken her vow to never go back to online dating. Apparently, four glasses were all it took to drown out the voice of reason. The proof was in her email inbox this morning: confirmation of registration to the Star-Crossed Dating Service.

At least she hadn't done it alone. She'd dragged Maggie and Gwen along with her on a quest for what the email promised would be an out-of-this-world dating experience.

"I could use a little out of this world," she mused to herself as she looked around. Vancouver was a beautiful city, but it was easy to forget that when you never got to compare it to anywhere else. Lisa had spent her whole life here, and she dreamed of taking off to explore the world someday. Someday was still a long way off, though, considering she barely earned enough money to eat and make her rent.

Lisa made her living drawing caricatures and quick sketches for tourists. It wasn't exactly a glamorous or high-paying job, especially when the tourists were few and far between. It was still early in the season, which meant the artists and street performers that dotted the seawall outnumbered their potential customers. She could head home to work on her paintings, but the spring sunshine was too nice to head indoors yet.

She sat underneath the canopy of her umbrella, idly sketching her surroundings when inspiration struck. She opened her sketch book to a fresh page and started drawing, the world around her fading away as she worked. Apart from the occasional pause to push her blonde hair back from her face, she stayed focused on the face taking shape on the paper.

Her mystery man had dark hair with a hint of curl in it, a strong jaw, and a mouth that curved up into an arrogant smile. Try as she might, she couldn't get his eyes right, though. She'd drawn them dark and brooding, staring back at her from beneath a lightly furrowed brow. She kept working at them, and then, in a flash of insight, she knew what was wrong. She reached out with a bare foot to snag the strap of her crocheted art supply bag and pulled it close enough that she could reach it without setting down the sketch book.

She fished out two of the artist's pens she used for signing her work and considered them for a moment. Gold or silver? She dropped the silver one back into her bag and quickly added a few gold highlights to her creation's eyes.

"Better." She stared at the face she'd drawn, wondering where her muse had drawn her inspiration from this time. It wasn't a face she recognized from television or the movies. And if she'd ever laid eyes on a man that good-looking in person, she'd damned sure wouldn't forget it. Especially not with those amazing eyes.

A breeze stirred, lifting her hair off her shoulders and ruffling the page of her book so that his eyes seemed to sparkle with silent amusement.

Lisa had long ago learned that when her muse took over like this, it was because the universe was trying to tell her something. Her friends teased her about it, but they knew it was true. After all, she'd drawn pictures of both Gwen and Maggie before they'd ever met. She'd drawn other things, too. Warnings that she had been too young and innocent to understand at the time. She wasn't innocent anymore, though. These days, when the universe whispered in her ear, she listened.

The wind came up again, lifting the hem of her skirt so that it swirled around her legs and sending goose bumps chasing down her spine. Something was coming. She stared down at the picture in her hands. Or *someone*.

2

———

Vadir made his way along the seawall, dodging tourists taking photos of themselves against the backdrop of the Pacific Ocean. It was early afternoon, and the sun had already turned the skin of many of the humans around him a painful shade of pink. Most of them seemed oblivious to their discomfort thanks to the wide array of sights and sounds that served as enticing distractions.

The city itself was noisy and crowded. In many ways, it was the same as a hundred other places he'd visited. It was clearly a hub of trade, with a bustling port system and a steady stream of visitors arriving to admire the natural beauty of the area.

He could make a killing here if he were allowed to initiate trade with this planet. Unfortunately, the Inter-planetary Council had very strict rules about contacting species before they had reached a certain level of development, and humans still had a long way to go.

As frustrating as it was to be denied a chance to make a profit, Vadir had to admit, he was enjoying his brief visit. The weather was pleasant, and the views were stunning. The air was laden with the scent of a myriad of tempting foods and confections, and there were any number of stalls and stations selling everything from artwork to jewelry.

Humans might be a primitive species in many respects, but they clearly had an appreciation for commerce.

In theory, the Council's rules made sense. The no-contact policy was meant to ensure that a species didn't acquire power and technology they weren't ready to use responsibly. It also meant some races, like Earthlings, were left to struggle with global issues that could have been easily resolved if they had the right tools. He had researched everything he could about this world, and it was entering a period of transition that not every species survived. Taking his mate away from here would be an act of kindness.

He still struggled to come to terms with that term: mate. If that's what this human female truly was. He'd read the report confirming that she carried Pyrosian DNA and gone through all the documentation that verified their compatibility. He still didn't believe she was his mate. His match, yes. The science all confirmed that he should be able to have children with this female, which was good news for his species. With only one female to every six men, the Pyrosian race was in danger of going extinct. But being compatible didn't mean she was his true *mate*. How could a female from the other side of the galaxy be his soul's other half, the one destined to unlock his abilities to manipulate fire? It didn't make any sense.

Not that it mattered. He was under orders to claim the human female and bring her to Pyros, and that was what he intended to do.

According to the limited amount of information that had been gathered about his supposed mate, she was an artist who spent the summer months selling her artwork to tourists somewhere along the seawall. She wouldn't have been contacted yet, but he wanted to see her. To watch and learn what he could before they met. He never entered negotiations until he had all the information he needed, and he didn't know enough about her. Not yet.

It was her laugh that drew his attention first. It wasn't a polite chortle but a full-throated exclamation of happiness. He turned to look for the source of such unfettered emotion, and there she was. Lisa Woods. The woman he had crossed a galaxy to meet.

She was perched on a small stool, making faces at a child as she sketched the boy and his parents. He couldn't see the drawing from this angle, but that didn't matter. Her talent wasn't what he'd come here to see.

It took a few minutes to find a vantage point that suited his purposes. He needed to watch without being noticed. A nearby vendor offered roasted tubes of meat wrapped in bread, and he purchased one, selecting several of the offered toppings at random before taking a seat nearby.

From here, he could observe and learn. She had an easy, approachable manner. A natural saleswoman, she made everyone she spoke to feel special. He could see it in the way they reacted to her. It didn't hurt that she was quite beautiful. Her pale blonde hair was loose around her shoulders despite the summer heat. Her multi-hued dress was light enough that every breath of wind made it swirl and flutter against her body, showing off her slender form and long legs.

He watched her for the next twenty minutes. By the time he finished eating the strange but tasty street food, he had discovered more than he'd learned in the hours he'd spent reading her files. Those had been the facts of her life. Useful in their own way, but none of them had prepared him for the vivacious energy and inherent gentleness of this female. Finding her price to leave with him would be a challenge, but spending time in her company would be no hardship at all.

He pulled his communicator out of his pocket and

punched in a brief request to the ship in orbit. It was time to initiate the match.

He rose from the bench and slipped back into the crowd, resisting the temptation to linger. Lisa would be getting an email soon, with his picture. He needed to be out of sight before that happened.

The next time he saw his future mate, he'd make his pitch and start negotiations. By this time tomorrow, he should have closed the deal and completed his mission. He was rich, powerful, and could offer her a life of luxury and safety. What female would say no to that?

Lisa was having her best day of the season so far. There were plenty of potential customers out enjoying the sun, and she'd already made enough to cover next month's rent, with a little extra to go into her rainy-day fund. She loved times like this. The energy of the people walking past was happy and upbeat, which in turn energized her and her muse. She was doing a brisk business, even selling two of her bigger pieces.

A break in the crowd finally gave her a chance to catch her breath and pull a peanut butter and banana sandwich out of her bag. She nibbled on her lunch while checking her phone for messages and emails. She was almost done when a new email popped up, and she read it with a gleeful squeal. After months of waiting, the dating site she and the others had signed up for had finally come online, and she had a match!

She didn't bother to read the terms and conditions. Instead, she scrolled to the bottom of the email and clicked the link to her match. "Please let him be cute. Please let him be cute."

"Hello, hotness." She stared at the image on her screen, then squealed in delight, crammed her sandwich in her mouth, and hopped off the stool to crouch beside her bag. She grabbed her sketch book, thumbing through the pages.

Gotcha.

Phone in one hand, sketch book in the other, Lisa compared the two likenesses. The only detail that differed was his eyes. His were dark brown instead of the gold she'd envisioned. She set the book aside and sat down again, happily nibbling on her sandwich while she read through the rest of the information on her mystery man's profile. His name was Vadir, and he was an entrepreneur with a wide range of corporate investments. She wrinkled her nose. Her match was a corporate suit-and-tie guy? How was that going to work?

She scrolled back up to his picture and took a better look. He wasn't wearing a suit in the photo. It was a dress shirt, unbuttoned at the throat. Well, at least he knew how to be a little unbuttoned already.

The rest, she'd just have to teach him. There was no doubt in her mind that she'd have the opportunity. His face in her sketch book proved they already had a connection. All that was left was for her to click the little button labeled "Accept Match."

A tap of her finger and it was done. "Alright, Mister Corporate hottie, tag, you're it."

She set the phone to vibrate and left it on her easel while she finished her lunch. She was still wiping the last traces of peanut butter off her fingers when the phone buzzed.

It couldn't be him already, could it? She checked to make sure there weren't any potential customers nearby and then grabbed her phone. She had a new message on the dating site.

"Hello. Couldn't be happier to know you accepted me as your match. I'm intrigued by your profile and entranced by your picture. I'm happy to communicate with you by email, but to be honest, I'd rather talk to you in person. Would you be interested in meeting me for dinner?"

No spelling mistakes. Complete sentences. No sexual innuendoes and he'd used multi-syllable words. Vadir had already managed to outperform eighty percent of her online dates, and they hadn't even met yet.

Why don't we do both? Chat now, meet for dinner later? Do you have time for that? Her heart was racing as she typed out her response and sent it.

The answer came back within seconds. *"For you, I'll make time. What would you like to chat about?"*

Wow. Feeling flushed and giddy, she typed out her answer. *"We should probably start by deciding where to meet for dinner. What's your favourite food?"*

While he was answering her question, Lisa called Maggie, eager to learn if she'd been matched, too. When it turned out she had, Lisa had bounced off her stool to do a victory dance right there on the seawall.

"You got one too? Who did you get? My guy is gorgeous. His name's Vadir, and he's stunning."

Maggie, ever the cautious one, confessed she hadn't clicked the link yet, which led to some cajoling and minor threats. Once she saw her match, Maggie was excited, too, even if she tried to hide it. Lisa knew her friend too well to buy the act. Maggie had a crunchy shell, but underneath, she was a gooey romantic who wanted what they all did--someone to share their lives with.

Once she was sure Maggie was on board, Lisa let her go and called Gwen. She was probably tucked away in her favourite corner of the used bookshop where she worked, reading through her lunch hour again. Gwen didn't pick up, another sure sign she was reading.

"Hey, Gwen. Call or text me when you get this. Just checking in to see if you got your match from Star-Crossed dating agency, yet. Maggie and I did, so the odds are good you got one, too. I hope yours is as hot as mine."

Two hours later, the wind was rising, and the ocean had turned from blue to greenish-grey, a sure sign that the weather was about to turn. The crowds had thinned, and Lisa decided it was time to head home.

She messaged Vadir to let him know she was finished work. They'd been messaging back and forth all afternoon, and the more they talked, the more Lisa wanted to meet him. He was smart, witty, and had asked her all sorts of questions about her instead of talking about himself.

"See you at six. Looking forward to continuing this conversation in person."

His message made her want to kick up her heels and dance. It was about time things started looking up for her and her friends. They'd been on the downside of Fortune's wheel for what felt like forever.

The three of them had met in foster care, forging a friendship that survived every test and trial the world had thrown at them. Gwen was the first real friend Lisa ever had. They had arrived at their first home within days of each other, both of them reeling from grief and loss. Lisa had still been wearing the same clothes she'd worn to her mother's funeral. They were the only ones she owned. The rest of her things had still been in an evidence locker, silent witnesses to her mother's violent murder at the hands of her husband, Lisa's father.

Gwen had lost her grandmother, the only family she had left in the world, and had only been in care for a week when Lisa was brought in. Lisa had recognized her on sight and run to hug the older girl. It didn't matter that they'd never met. Lisa had sketched her face more than once, and she knew in her heart that this girl was destined to be her friend. Maggie had come into their lives a year later, and their little trio had been born.

Thoughts of Gwen had her checking her phone again. She had to have checked her messages at least once by now. There was only one reason her friend would have gone radio silent. Lisa sighed and looked skyward. "Come on, universe. Just once, couldn't you let all three of us be happy at the same time?"

She packed up her homemade bike trailer a little faster, the need to get home and talk to Gwen pushing Vadir and their date to the back of her mind. Gwen wouldn't want to ruin her friends' good news, so she was probably already home, baking up a storm and trying to pretend it didn't bother her that she hadn't been matched. Gwen would see it as more proof that she was destined to be alone. As her thirty-fifth birthday loomed, Lisa could almost see her friend's hopes for a family fade away.

Lisa still lived like she was in her twenties, and it was only recently that she'd felt any inclination to change that. It had been a gradual thing, but somewhere in the past year she'd stopped having short term flings and started looking for something more. So far, she'd come up short, which is why she'd joined Star-Crossed Dating Service.

The sky was darkening by the time she got home, and she pedaled the last few feet just as the first fat raindrops started to fall. She stashed her bike and trailer in the shed, locked it up, and made a run for the house she shared with her two best friends.

The scent of fresh-baked cookies was the only clue she needed to know where Gwen was the second she walked through the door.

Shaking the last stray raindrops from her hair, Lisa headed down the shared hallway until she reached Gwen's door. Their living arrangement was a little different, but it worked. Each of them had their own suite on different floors. Lisa lived upstairs, Gwen had the main floor, and Maggie claimed the basement.

"Hey, cookie momma, I'm coming in."

"It's open."

Lisa opened the door and was enveloped in a fragrant cloud of sugar, chocolate, and cinnamon. Racks of cooling cookies covered the small kitchen table, and there was even a tray of brownies sitting on the counter. "I'd ask if you were okay, but I can see you're not. Cookies *and* brownies? How bad a day are you having?"

Gwen groaned and gestured around her. "There's an apple pie in the oven, too. Does that answer your question?"

"Oh man. That's bad."

"They're closing the bookstore. Jeff says he just can't afford to lose any more money.

We close the doors at the end of the month, but Jeff offered to keep me on to help him pack up and get the place ready to sell. But I'm going to be out work soon."

"Shit. No wonder you're baking. You've had that job for what, ten years? That store is like your second home."

Gwen nodded and wiped her eyes with a corner of the brightly patterned floral apron she was wearing. "I'll find something else, but I don't think it'll be the same. That was the one thing in my life I was good at, you know?"

"You're good at so much more than selling books."

"I'm thirty-five years old, and all I know how to do is read and run a cash register. I can't even get a date right now. How am I going to find a job in this economy?"

Lisa winced. "No dates? So, you didn't get an email from Star-Crossed like Maggie and I did?"

"Oh, I got an email. Basically, it said thank you for your interest, but there's no match in our database for you at this time as *they are catering to a younger age group*. At least I'll get the money, they're mailing me a cheque. I'm going to need it."

"They said you were too *old*? You're only two years older than me! How can they say that? You're young, gorgeous, and amazing. I'm going to email and tell them they made a mistake."

Gwen shook her head, making her black curls bounce slightly. "Don't. Whatever they're looking for, I'm not it. I'm okay with that. Not every guy wants a borderline spinster with a double helping of curves. I'll just have to look for my forever guy somewhere else. I haven't given up on him, but I wish he'd get here soon."

Lisa wished her friend could see herself the way others did. She was beautiful, inside and out, but Gwen couldn't see it. "Your forever guy is out there. I know it."

"Forget me and my non-existent love life. Show me the guy they matched you with."

"Which one do you want to see, the picture they sent me today, or the drawing I made of him months ago?"

Gwen's mouth fell open. "You drew him? But you only do that when...Oh my god. Show me both!"

They talked for another twenty minutes, and when she left to get ready for her date, Gwen had stopped baking and was starting to clean up her kitchen, which Lisa took as a good sign.

Soon, the three of them would have a girls' night in and make sure that Gwen was truly okay. She'd have to check with Maggie and find out when she had a free night.

As she made her goodbyes, Gwen tucked a baggie full of cookies into her hand. "If the date goes badly, they're good comfort food."

"What if it goes really well?"

Her dark eyes gleamed with amusement. "Then they'll be a great high energy snack between rounds of mind-blowing sex. I'm living vicariously through you, so have fun!"

Lisa nodded and dashed upstairs to get ready for her date. Tonight was going to be something special, she could feel it. The only thing darkening her mood was the fact that Gwen wasn't sharing in their good fortune. Sometimes, the universe was grossly unfair.

3

———

Vadir knew the moment his date arrived. The conversations around him hushed, and every male in the restaurant turned to watch her cross the room. She wore a dark red dress that skimmed over her slender curves and fell only halfway down her thigh, revealing her long, toned legs. Her shoes were unlike anything he had seen before. There was little to them except for a bit of leather over her toes, and the heels were several inches high and incredibly narrow. The effect was alluring, but he wasn't sure how she managed to walk in them with such grace.

It wasn't until Lisa got closer that he heard a faint, musical chime that seemed to match her stride. It took him a moment to spot the reason; she was wearing a delicate chain hung with tiny, silver bells around one ankle.

He didn't recall anything like that being mentioned in the files and research he'd been provided with via cognitive augmentation. Of course, there hadn't been enough time to do a full study of the diverse cultures and practices of the human species, so maybe this was common courtship attire for the females.

He stood and crossed the floor to meet her, and she smiled as she recognized him.

"Vadir?" Her voice was a light, soothing alto that flowed like cool water over parched rock.

"Hello, Lisa. It's nice to meet you." He held out his hand and was stunned when she ignored it, walking right up to him and giving him a hug instead. Even more surprising than the embrace was the blue spark that arced from her hand to his shoulder as she reached for him. He barely caught a glimpse of it, but the sizzling impact of the shock that accompanied the Spark was all the confirmation he needed. This female wasn't simply his match, she was his mate. By the Flames of the First One, she was the real thing!

"It's nice to meet you, too." She stepped back to smile at him, her crystalline blue eyes bright with interest. "Look at that. One hug, and we've already got sparks flying."

"Indeed." He offered her his hand again, willing himself to calmness despite the storm raging within. "Shall we go to our table and order drinks?"

"That sounds like a good place to start." She took

his hand, and it felt like the most natural thing in the world to walk back to their table with their fingers interlocked, despite the fact he'd never done it before. He had always kept his personal relationships out of the public eye.

He had regained at least some of his wits by the time they were seated. His plans hadn't changed, but the timeline had. That spark, *the* Spark, meant the Scorching had begun. With every minute that passed, the mating fever would grow stronger. Soon, he would be at the whim of his desires, and so would Lisa. He needed to explain a great deal before that happened.

Once they were seated, a waiter appeared to take their drink order, giving Vadir a few more seconds to gather his wits.

"I'm going to start with the obvious question, first. Why would someone with your looks and resume need to apply to a matchmaking site to get a date?" Lisa asked the moment they were alone.

Direct. He liked that. "I don't need help getting a date. I signed up because I'm looking for something more meaningful and I haven't been able to find it on my own. I'm guessing you're here for the same reason. You are far too lovely to be lacking male attention."

"I always thought I'd find someone without having to look for him, but..." she shrugged. "I'm in my thirties, now. Since I don't seem to be having any luck finding someone special, I thought I'd try something different. My friends signed up, too. We're sort of doing this together."

"I have a friend who signed up, as well." Vadir briefly wondered how Joran was doing with his match. Had they met, yet? Had he found his true mate, too?

"Has he had any luck?"

"Not sure. I haven't talked to him recently. I was distracted by a lovely woman's photo and texts." The truth of that statement made him grin. He hadn't been distracted by anyone or anything in years. Not until today.

"I was happily distracted by our chat, too. I'm glad you made time to talk with me. It made meeting you tonight less nerve-wracking."

"It was the same for me."

They paused their conversation while their waiter returned with their drinks and took their meal order. Vadir didn't bother trying the wine he'd ordered. He was more curious about the woman sitting across from him. His interest in her was growing rapidly, and he knew it was more than her looks and charm. The Scorching was starting. Alcohol would only accelerate the process, and he was already on a tight deadline. By the time dinner was over, he needed to have this deal done or risk losing control.

He never lost control.

"So, what exactly do you do? What kind of company do you run?" she asked.

"I'm in trade. My business is mostly about making connections between buyers and sellers. I find new markets and set up distribution systems. Sometimes I maintain ownership, but often I sell my share and invest the money in a new market somewhere else."

"You must travel a lot," Lisa said. Her voice sounding wistful.

"All over the gal—globe." He caught himself before the word galaxy crossed his lips, but only barely. It was growing harder to focus on anything but the beautiful female sitting just beyond his reach. Was her skin as soft as it looked? Would her lips taste of wine if he kissed her right now? Flame and fury, he was tempted to find out.

Belatedly he recalled that her profile had mentioned that she wanted to travel and he added. "What about you? Do you get to travel much? Your profile mentioned that you wanted to see new places."

"I've never been further than Seattle. The spirit is willing, but the wallet..." she shook her head. "Unless I find a patron or get lucky with a gallery show someday, travel isn't likely to be in the cards for me."

"Where would you go if you could afford it?" he asked, curious.

"Anywhere in the world?" Her eyes lit up.

"Anywhere at all."

"Greece. Or Spain. Or Italy. Maybe all of them.

Yeah, definitely all of them." She laughed. "Is that greedy?"

"Why those places? And no, I don't think it's greedy. It's a big world out there." A world she would soon be leaving behind forever. He'd have to show her the wonders of Pyros, instead.

"I want to visit the cities where some of the true masters learned to be artists. To sit in little restaurants, eat the same food they did, listen to the same languages, immerse myself in another culture and then try and capture it all in my art."

"And then what? Sell your artwork there? Is there a demand for the work of artists from other countries?"

Her brow furrowed. "Then nothing. I'd stay as long as I could, then come home again. I might be able to sell a few pieces and extend my stay, but eventually, I'd come home. This is where my life is. My friends. I want to see the world, but I don't want to stay gone forever."

"Why not? One place is really like another, isn't it?"

This time she didn't frown, she stared at him in outright confusion. "Of course it isn't. When you come back from your travels, don't you feel better for being home? Back to the one place where you have friends and family and well...everything that really matters to you?"

"I have residences on several pla—in several places." He shrugged. "They all feel about the same to me."

"So, you don't have a place you consider home? What about your family?"

"I have no family." The words came easily after all this time. A simple statement of fact, nothing more.

"Oh." Instead of looking uncomfortable or spouting an empty platitude, she reached out and covered his hand with hers. "Me either. But I made a family of my own. Friends that are more like sisters. Isn't there anyone in your life like that? Or are you alone as well as homeless?"

"I'm not homeless. And yes, I have friends." He turned his hand over to take hold of hers and tried to ignore the surge of desire that slammed into him at that simple touch.

"I grew up in foster care. I know the difference between having a place to live and having a real home. If you had a home, you'd know the difference, too."

He considered that for a moment, surprised to realize that she was right. After his father's death, he'd been shuttled between relatives. Once he was old enough to take care of himself, he had always lived alone. And not one of the places he lived had ever felt like home.

Before he could admit to that, his phone chimed at the same time the communicator in his pocket vibrated softly. Unwilling to let go of Lisa's hand, he managed to pull out the phone with his off hand and check the screen. It was Commander Denza. If he was trying to reach him right now, it was important.

"You need to answer that, don't you?" Lisa asked.

"I should." He looked up to find her looking at him with an expression of amused understanding.

"Go deal with your empire. I'm not going anywhere. But if you take too long, I'm eating all the breadsticks." She was smiling as she shooed him off with a wave of her hand.

He rose to his feet without letting go of her hand, bringing to his lips for a brief kiss before releasing her again. "I won't be long. You're the only important thing on my agenda tonight."

He found a quiet corner where he could speak in private and contacted Kash, voice contact only. "You're interrupting a life-changing moment. What is it?"

Kash chuckled. "Not you, too? The prince has reported that he has his mate with him, and the Scorching has been initiated. I thought to warn you it was possible."

"You're a bit late with that information. I've also experienced the Spark with my match."

"How long do you have?"

Vadir sighed. "Not as long as I would like. We're still conversing in the middle of a very public eating establishment. I can hardly drag her out of here and teleport her back to my ship like a Romaki barbarian without explaining matters to her."

There was a brief pause. "The prince found it necessary to do just that. You might want to move things along quickly, or risk having to make the same choice."

"Joran *took* his mate? The queen will set his hair on fire when she finds out."

"He claims he had no other choice."

Vadir considered that for a moment and decided it was time he returned to Lisa. He didn't want to be faced with the same choice as Joran. Not if he could avoid it. "I'll try to avoid that outcome. Unlike his Highness, I have some experience with high-level negotiations."

Kash chuckled. "Then I'll wish you luck and leave you to it."

Vadir tucked his communicator away and headed back to his table. It was time to set the next stage of his plan in motion.

4

____

Lisa watched her date walk away and took note that the back of him looked as good as the front did. Broad shoulders, trim waist, and when she had hugged him she'd gotten a good feel for the muscular body he was hiding beneath his hand-tailored shirt. She had enough friends who did cosplay and costuming to recognize a hand-crafted garment. Nothing he had on was an off-the-rack purchase. At least, nothing she'd seen so far.

She sipped her wine and sorted through her first impressions. He was gorgeous. Well mannered, and clearly intelligent. He was also in dire need of someone to loosen him up a little. What kind of man could think one place was the same as another? Even in Vancouver, different parts of the city had their own flavour and pace.

Lisa recognized his type, though. Years in the system had taught her that most children had one of two responses to losing their parents. They either shut themselves down and tried to control the world-- and their grief--in any way they could, or they went wild and pushed every boundary they could find. He was clearly the first type. She'd taken the wild path, hurling herself into new experiences just to try and feel something that wasn't grief.

She was one of the lucky ones. Her friends had been there to stop her from doing anything too reckless. They had both closed down in their grief, and while they helped to ground her, she was coaxing them back into the world. Lisa believed her mother had guided her grief-stricken daughter towards the two souls that could help her heal and keep her safe after she was gone.

Smiling, Lisa chuckled to herself before taking another sip of her wine. Her mom was probably the reason she was out on this date in the first place. Even from the other side, she was still trying to do her best for the daughter she had died protecting. When she was alive, her mom had taught her to be strong and self-reliant. She hadn't wanted Lisa to make the same mistakes she'd made. *You've got to trust in yourself, baby. Don't let anyone tell you how to live your life, or what you're worth.*

Her mother hadn't chosen well for herself. Lisa's

father was a jealous, violent son of a bitch who had hunted down his wife and killed her because he believed he had the right.

"Nice pick, Mom. Smart, hot, a gentleman, and gainfully employed. But really, a suit and tie guy? It's like you don't know me at all."

A second later a pulse of heat bloomed deep in her chest. For a second it was as if she was standing in front of an open kiln, and then the sensation was gone. *And that's what I get for trying to argue with my mother instead of accepting that she knows what she's doing.*

Another sip of her chilled white wine banished the last of the strange warmth, though she was feeling the effects faster than usual. She felt mildly tipsy already. Probably because she hadn't eaten anything since lunch. Time to make good on her threat to eat all the breadsticks. She'd taken her first bite when a stranger's voice interrupted.

"Now this is a tragedy. A beautiful woman dining alone."

Lisa glanced up to see a blond, heavily tanned man a few years older than her standing at her elbow. He was dressed in the standard uniform of every travelling businessman she'd ever seen: a creased and rumpled dress shirt and a red and blue striped tie that was slightly askew.

"I'm not alone. My date had to step away for a moment. He'll be back any minute."

"Honey, you can do better 'n him. If I had a beauty like you sitting across from me, I wouldn't leave you alone for a second." The blond plonked himself down into Vadir's empty chair with a sly grin. "See? Now you're with me. I'm Mike, your date for the rest of the evening."

"My name isn't honey, and you are most certainly not *with* me. I'd like you to go away, now. You're interrupting my dinner date."

The blond snorted. "I don't see your date or any dinner. Why don't you relax and talk with me until one or the other of those things makes an appearance? You might decide to change your mind."

The jerk reminded Lisa of her father. The bravado, the disrespectful way he spoke to her. He made her uneasy, and she wanted him gone. "I'm not going to change my mind. You need to go, now."

Of course, the bastard didn't listen to her. He grabbed one of the breadsticks and broke it in two, sending bits of crust flying across the tabletop. "Why would I go when we're having such a nice chat?"

She eyed her glass of wine and briefly considered tossing the contents in the asshole's face, but she knew better. Escalating the situation wasn't in her best interest. Mike was bigger, stronger, and she had no doubt that he'd had enough to drink that he wouldn't hesitate to retaliate if she pushed him too far.

"We're not chatting. You sat down uninvited and

started harassing me. Now, I'm asking you to please leave me the hell alone!" She raised her voice so that the people seated nearby all heard what she said. None of them reacted beyond a few uncomfortable glances in her direction.

Cowards. She was on her own.

"No need to get bitchy, hon. How about you pull those claws back in and behave?"

She ignored his taunt. She knew how bullies operated and had long ago learned how to deal with them. Be strong. Be confident. Be ready to run if necessary. She carefully toed off her high-heeled shoes, then laid her hands flat on the table and leaned in. "You haven't seen bitchy, yet. But if you don't leave right now, you're going to."

His eyes widened, and for a moment she thought her message had finally gotten through his thick skull, but then a hand touched her shoulder.

"Lisa, are you alright?"

Vadir was back. Mike hadn't been reacting to her at all. The jerk only cared that her date had returned.

She glanced up at Vadir and offered him a tight smile. "I'm okay."

He squeezed her shoulder gently, keeping his hand in place as he took a step toward Mike. "You're in my seat."

Mike gave him an insincere grin. "You can't blame a

man for trying. You shouldn't leave a beauty like that alone so long."

"Oh, I do blame you. There's no honour in poaching on another man's turf. She's with me."

The booze-addled fool turned red and started to bluster, but Vadir cut him off with a sharp gesture. "I think it's time you went back to your friends." He nodded towards a small group of middle-aged men huddled over their drinks, all of them watching the confrontation with interest.

"Yeah, fine. Whatever. She's not worth any more of my time, anyway." Mike lumbered to his feet.

Vadir's fingers tightened on her shoulder, and his voice lowered to a dangerous rumble. "Apologize to my fe—to Lisa. Now."

Mike turned a darker shade of red, and his blood-shot eyes narrowed to slits.

Vadir let go of her and stepped between herself and Mike. She got to her feet, ready to get out of the way if things got violent.

"Apologize, and then you can go buy you and your buddies a drink." Vadir reached into his pocket and pulled out a money clip heavy with bills. He peeled off several and tossed them onto the table in front of Mike.

Mike's gaze dropped to the table, his anger losing out to greed. "Sure. I'm sorry I bothered the little lady."

It wasn't much of an apology, but she'd take it if it meant the ass finally left her alone.

"Her name is Lisa." Vadir interrupted Mike as he reached for the cash.

"Huh? Fine. Yeah. I'm sorry I bothered you, Lisa." Mike grabbed the money and left, weaving unsteadily between the tables.

Vadir turned to look at her, his expression solemn. "I'm sorry. I should not have left you alone. I had thought this would be a safe location, but it appears I was wrong." He glanced around at the nearby tables. "I cannot believe that no one came to your aid."

She shrugged. "People don't like to get involved in someone else's drama. I appreciate that you did. Get involved, I mean."

His expression softened, and for a second his eyes seemed to flash a bright gold. "Of course I'd get involved. You're my fe—my date."

That was the second time he'd changed his phrasing at the last minute. Before this night ended, she planned on finding out what he was almost saying. Something told her it was important.

"Would you like to continue our date here, or would you prefer we moved to another location, away from them?" Distaste dripped from the last word as he gestured vaguely to where Mike and the others were seated.

"I'm happy to stay here, but only if you promise not to leave me alone for too long the next time something comes up."

Vadir pulled out her chair and helped her sit, then took his seat and pulled out his phone. He made a show of turning it off, then put it away again with a smile that made her pulse race. "No more distractions, I promise. I'm all yours."

They made their orders and started talking again. It took a while for Lisa to relax again, but Vadir's charm and attention helped. He asked her about her work, her goals, and more about her dreams of travelling. By the time the appetizers arrived, she was enjoying herself again.

"I've talked enough. Tell me something about yourself," she prompted him.

"What would you like to know?"

"What's your worst bad habit?"

He gave her another of his sinful smiles, reaching across the table to stroke his fingers over the back of her hand. "I've got more than one. One of the perks to being rich, I can afford to indulge myself from time to time."

"Tell me one of them."

He was quiet for a moment and his expression changed from flirtatious to serious. "I think my worst habit is that I work too much."

That wasn't the answer she'd been expecting. It was surprisingly honest.

"Why do you do that?"

"Because I don't like to delegate. I need to be in control."

There was that control issue again. Why had her mother and the universe picked someone like him? She wanted to like him. Hell, she *did* like him. But...

"Do you think you could ever find a reason to stop?"

His gaze met hers, and the heat in his made her ache and tingle on the most interesting places.

"I think I might have found one. Now, I have to convince her to come away with me."

She felt like she'd been dropped into the middle of a furnace. Licks of flame danced across her skin where he touched her, and a searing heat blossomed deep in her chest.

"Where would I be going?"

"With me. I told you, I travel a great deal." He closed his hand around hers. "I'd like you to consider coming with me."

Stunned to speechlessness, Lisa could only gape at him.

He pressed on. "You'd have every luxury imaginable. The best of everything."

"But my friends are here. It's the height of tourist season. I need to be working. I can't run away with you." She flashed him a smile. "Even if I am very tempted."

"You want to stay here and work? I thought you wanted to travel. This is your chance, Lisa. I promise I can show you places and wonders you've never dreamed of."

"And it sounds amazing. But I'm not running away with a man I barely know just because he offers me money and adventure."

He looked at her with bewilderment. "But you signed up for the Star-Crossed Dating Agency. I'm offering you exactly what you signed up for, an out-of-this-world adventure."

"Ask me again when we know each other better."

"I don't need to know you better to recognize the bond between us. Can't you feel it? It's like a star is burning inside me right now."

She pulled her hand away from his. "I don't feel anything like that." She was lying, but there was no way in hell she was admitting to that and fueling whatever delusion Vadir was under. He might be sexy and rich, but that didn't mean she was going to fall at his feet and let him take her away from her life and her friends.

"I think you do. You must." He ran a hand through his hair, rumpling the perfect style. "Scorching," He muttered the word so softly she barely heard it.

"Maybe you have a fever. Are you sick?" That might explain his strange behaviour.

He gave her an odd smile. "Oh, I definitely have a fever, but I'm not sick."

"I think maybe we should call a raincheck on this date, then. If you've got a fever, then you need to go home and rest. You can text me when you're feeling better."

"What I need is to find out what would tempt you to come away with me. I have to leave in a few days, and I want you to be with me when I do."

She was still trying to find something to say when she was saved by the arrival of their entrees. He was making her uncomfortable, and she decided she needed a few minutes alone to decide what she was going to do about it.

The moment the server left, she stood and gave Vadir her sweetest smile. "I need to wash my hands before I eat. Sorry, I should have done it sooner, but I got distracted by our conversation."

He rose as soon as she did in an old-school display of manners that would have made her smile if she wasn't already feeling off-balance. "Do you want me to escort you?"

She glanced over to the table where Mike and his buddies had been sitting. The space was empty. "No, I'll be fine. Be right back."

She managed to subtly snag her purse as she left, but by the time she remembered her shoes, she was a few feet away from the table and didn't feel like going back in case Vadir started pushing her again.

The restrooms were down a long, dimly lit hall.

She passed the men's room, then the ladies', and claimed a corner of the hall beside the emergency exit. She could call Gwen, but Gwen would insist on coming down to get her, and Lisa didn't want to ask that of her friend. She wasn't totally sure she wanted to end the date, either.

Vadir was clearly used to getting what he wanted, but he'd also showed her that he could be vulnerable. He was smart, sexy, charming, and despite what she'd said to him, she was powerfully attracted to him...even if he was pushy and possibly a little nuts. To be fair, more than one guy had said the same thing about her.

Losing her mother had taught her that life was too short to be held back by fear. Fear had stopped her mom from leaving her abusive bastard of a husband for years. That was time she'd never get back. Sometimes, Lisa felt like she was living for not just herself, but for her mom, too.

Her musings were interrupted by loud voices coming out of the men's room. Familiar voices. Damn and double damn, that sounded like Mike.

"...the women in this city are fucking bitches. All of 'em. Won't give a man the time of day without checking your credit rating first."

The door started to open, and the voices got louder. With nowhere else to go, she turned and bolted through the emergency exit. She would have been fine, but the damned thing was alarmed, and a shrill beeping filled her ears as her feet hit the cool, wet concrete of the alley.

Back alleys and bare feet. She was going to need a tetanus shot after this.

She kept moving, trying to avoid the bigger puddles and hoping that the light drizzle didn't soak her too badly before she made it back into the restaurant. She was still in the alley when the back door flew open again. She looked back, prepared to run if it was Mike or one of his idiot friends.

"Lisa!" Vadir appeared in the alley, looking a little frantic. When he saw her, he ran over to her at a speed that made her wonder if he 'd been a track star when he was younger.

Once he was closer, he slowed to a walk, not stopping until they were almost touching. "You left. Why?"

"I needed a minute to think about what you were saying. Before that happened, I crossed paths with Mike again. I ended up out here, but I was coming back. I just needed to walk around to the front door. Why did you follow me?"

He frowned. "I went looking for you when I heard the alarm. I was concerned. Wait, you left the table because of me?"

"I did." She opted for the truth. "My father was a possessive, abusive bastard who ended up killing my mother while I hid in a closet. I don't react well to possessive or pushy men."

"I'm sorry about your mother. As for being possessive…" He grunted in frustration. "There's a lot I need to explain to you. Time isn't on our side right now. When that drunken fool accosted you, I lost my head a little. Where I'm from, no male would do what he did. It's not acceptable to treat a female that way."

"Well, you're clearly not from around here, then, because that happens a lot." She shrugged. "If things had escalated, I would have dealt with him."

He gave her a look an incredulous look, his brows lifted almost to his hairline. "What would you have done, stab him with the heel of your shoe?" His gaze dropped to her feet, and he frowned. "Where are your shoes?"

"I left them back at the restaurant. I kicked them off in case I needed to move quickly and forgot to put them back on afterward." Despite everything, she laughed. "You're right. I should have used one as a weapon. I'll remember that for next time."

For a second, she could have sworn Vadir's eyes flashed that brilliant gold again.

"There will not be a next time. I will not leave you alone again. Each time I do so, you seem to find trouble," he said, his voice a sexy rumble that wrapped around her heart and made her clit throb in time to her heartbeat.

"I'm telling you, I saw her again. The uptight

blonde with the great tits." Another male voice came out of the darkness"

Another male answered, but his comment was too slurred to be understood.

"Fuck you. I'm not obsessed or delusional. I saw her go through the door right as the alarm went off."

"You have got to be fucking kidding me. Three times in one night?" Lisa hissed in frustration and glanced over at Vadir, her finger to her lips to remind him to speak softly. "We should probably hide, in case he decides to look for me. I don't want you getting into a fight, and I left my attack heels inside."

He frowned. "You don't want me to fight? Do you think I'm incapable of defending you?"

"What? No. I'm sure you take some sort of kick-boxing class or weekend warrior boot camp to have a body like yours. You said time isn't on our side. How much of it do you want to waste punching that jerk in the face?"

"Gotta take a leak. Be back in three shakes of my tallywacker." Mike was laughing to himself as he staggered into sight at the end of the alley.

"I'm not letting him near you again." Vadir moved so quickly she didn't have time to react. One second she was standing in the rain-soaked alley, and the next she was being lifted into his arms.

"Vadir! What the hell are you doing? Put me down."

"No. You're not safe here. The males of your species are barbaric, and you don't wish me to fight to protect you. Flames and fury, you don't even have shoes on your feet right now. You clearly need someone to take care of you."

She started to thrash and kick, determined to get free. "I can take care of myself. Put me down right now, or you're going to learn that first hand."

"I can't do that. We're nearly out of time, and I can't risk us being interrupted again." He shifted her in his arms and touched his left wrist. "Hang on. This isn't going to be pleasant."

"What won't be—" her question was cut off by a strident squeal that pierced her to the marrow of her bones. It went on for several agonizing seconds then ended as abruptly as it started, leaving her adrift in an abyss of nothingness.

There was no light or sound. Absolutely darkness pressed in from all directions. She tried to scream and discovered she had no voice. Worse, she had no body. No breath. No lungs. Just when she started to wonder if she would ever escape the hellish darkness, the world returned in a blast of light and noise. Her senses reeled, and she struggled to make sense of what she was seeing. None of it made any sense. *Where the hell am I?*

5

The dark alley Lisa had been standing in was gone. Hell, she wasn't even outside anymore. Wherever they were, it was warm, dry, and brightly lit. Stark white walls curved in a semi-circle behind them, forming a small alcove. Beyond she could see a console full of instruments and two seats. It looked a bit like an airplane cockpit.

Overwhelmed by the number of things she couldn't explain, she focused on the one thing she could deal with: Vadir.

She jammed her feet against one curved wall of the alcove and shoved as hard as she could. It was enough to loosen his hold, and she pressed her advantage. She pushed, kicked and twisted until he finally released her, though he was careful enough that she landed on her feet instead of falling into a heap on the floor.

"What was that? What did you do to me? And where the fuck are we?" She demanded, waving her hands around her in wild gestures. She knew she was losing it, and she really didn't care.

"That was a short-range teleportation. I brought you to my ship where we can talk without interruption."

"As much as I wish it were otherwise, teleportation is not a real thing." She poked her index finger into the rock-hard planes of his chest. "Try again. And this time don't use any words you learned from watching Star Trek or Harry Potter."

He captured her hand in his, pinning it to his chest. "This is real. We're on my ship, the Redshift 7. We got here by teleporting. You're my true mate, and I'm here to negotiate an agreement with you and then take you back to Pyros with me."

She yanked her hand out of his grip and stepped away from him. "I'm not negotiating with you, and I'm not going anywhere but home. Alone. Right now. Which way is the door?" She started looking around, but the markings on the walls were all in an unfamiliar script, and there didn't appear to be any doorways, just a stretch of corridor with occasional panels on the walls to her right, and the cockpit-like area to her left.

He followed her out of the alcove, but instead of arguing with her, he started speaking in a sharp, tongue-twisting series of syllables. She didn't recognize a single thing he said, and she started to wonder if he wasn't crazy, after all. The number of things she couldn't explain were stacking up fast.

The fire of her anger met the first icy tendrils of pure panic, pushing her to her breaking point.

"Where's the door, Vadir? Stop babbling and answer me!"

Another voice started speaking in that same strange language, and then the floor beneath her feet began to vibrate and hum as if an engine had started. An engine meant movement and movement meant— oh hell no.

Vadir stepped into the cockpit and gestured toward a seat. "You're not leaving until I've had a chance to explain things. I'm truly sorry, this is not how I intended things to go. I promise we'll talk just as soon as I find us a quiet spot where we won't be detected."

"Let me out of here right now." Her voice was more of a cracked whisper than the battle cry she was hoping for.

"I can't do that."

The last shreds of her control snapped, and she exploded. With a frustrated snarl, she closed the short distance between them and shoved him. "I want to go home!"

He grunted, more in surprise than pain and she followed up her push with a punishing right hook.

Still off balance from her initial shove, Vadir staggered backward, missing the two chairs and landing rather heavily on top of the console. That's when all hell broke loose. Alarms wailed, lights strobed, and the floor dropped out from under her. She screamed and tried to find something to hang onto, but there was nothing but the slick surface of the wall within her reach.

She experienced the next few seconds as if she were watching it in slow motion. Vadir pushed himself off the console and caught her as she slid down the sloped floor toward him. She expected him to at least be annoyed at her, but all he did was shove her into the nearest of the chairs and somehow get her arms into a safety harness.

His eyes were glowing gold again as he locked gazes with her, his hands gripping the arms of her chair as the scream of the alarms grew to an ear-shattering crescendo. She recognized his expression, and it made her heart twist. She had seen that look of grim determination on her mother's face just before she closed the closet door and went to face Lisa's father for the last time.

She reached for him, managing to cup his face in her hand for a brief second before the wild ride ended with a sickening crash.

The pain of the straps biting into her shoulders roused Lisa from her dazed stupor. The floor was angled downward on the left, the angle steep enough to pull her partially out of her chair so that her left leg and arm were dangling at an uncomfortable angle.

She cautiously checked herself for damage. Apart from feeling like she'd been tossed into a jumbo-sized tumble dryer, she didn't appear to have any serious injuries. She ached all over, and her ears were still ringing, but that was the worst of it. She wriggled out of the harness that had saved her.

A few amber and red lights flickered on the console in front of her. She had no idea what they might mean, but they did provide a little light in the otherwise dark space.

"Vadir?"

No answer.

"Dammit. You better not be hurt. I need you alive and awake, so I can yell at you for abducting me...and then thank you for saving my life." He'd put her in that harness knowing full well he wouldn't have time to save himself.

She managed to get to her feet, hanging on to the chair for balance as she braced one foot against the wall and kept the other on the floor. A quick scan confirmed that Vadir wasn't in the cockpit with her. She would have been able to see him. *Damn it. Where is he?*

Gingerly she dropped to her hands and knees and started crawling in the other direction. The chimes on her ankle jingled as she crept along, the whimsical sound oddly incongruent with her current surroundings.

She nearly jumped out of her skin when a voice started speaking in that strange language again. It sounded remarkably calm, and it didn't take long for Lisa to realize that it had to be the ship's computer. Nothing alive could possibly be that cool after what they'd all experienced.

"It would be too much to hope that you speak English, wouldn't it?" she muttered.

"I am programmed to speak your language, yes."

"Terrific. In that case, uh...tell me where Vadir is and if he's even alive, call for help, and then give me a damage report or at least tell me we're not going to blow up."

"Vadir is alive and located three meters ahead and to your right. I am not programmed to obey operational commands from unregistered passengers." The sexless voice paused for a moment before adding. "But I can tell you that I do not believe there is any risk of explosion. I am a top of the line luxury cruise liner designed and built by the renowned engineers of the Caspar Shipyards. I am too well constructed to blow up."

"Good to know." Lisa kept crawling in the direction the computerized voice had indicated.

Less than a minute later, she was kneeling at Vadir's side. He was bleeding from a gash on his forehead, and there were several bruises blooming on his face and neck. He was unconscious, too, which wasn't a good sign. "Hey, computer—ship thingy. Can you scan Vadir and tell me if he's injured?"

"Of course. And you may call me Cas."

"Okay, Cas. I'm Lisa. Now, how's our patient?"

"His current condition is less than ideal. However, he has no broken bones or life-threatening injuries. I am equipped with a fully automated medical bay powered by a protected power supply. If you bring him there, I will be able to repair him."

She eyed Vadir's big body, then surveyed the sloped floor and the long stretch of corridor. "It would take an Olympic weightlifter to move this guy anywhere. I can't do it alone." Lisa sat down on the slanted floor and gently eased Vadir's head into her lap. She placed a hand over his cut and applied pressure, hoping it would at least slow the bleeding.

If anyone had asked her why she was helping the man who had just kidnapped her, she wouldn't have been able to give them a reason. She should be trying to escape, but her heart wasn't letting her leave.

"You owe me big time, Vee. I should leave your

sexy, unconscious ass here on the floor after what you did."

He groaned and muttered something in his strange language.

"And once you're awake, we are going to have a long talk about the shit you left out of your profile. You're not even the same species as me! And while I'm thrilled to discover I was right and aliens do exist, you're still not forgiven for lying to me. Or zapping me here. I hope your species knows what grovelling is, because you owe me a lot of it."

His eyes opened, and relief coursed through her as he cracked a ghost of a smile. "It's a good thing I'm rich, then. As I understand it, grovelling can be expensive. So, I take it we lived? Well, that's one thing that's gone right since I met you."

The pain he felt was nothing compared to the immense relief he experienced when he first heard Lisa's voice. She was alright. If his actions had led to her being hurt, he would have never forgiven himself.

"We lived. Which means you have a lot of explaining to do." Her lovely eyes were dark with worry, and it made him feel better than it should to know that concern was all for him.

"I do. I also owe you an apology." He reached up to

touch her cheek, and a blast of desire swept through him with the force of a comet strike. He had to fight the urge to drive his fingers into her hair and pull her in for a kiss. Flames, he needed to kiss her soon.

"Your eyes kept doing this weird colour shift from brown to gold. Why is that?"

"It's the Scorching." He tried to raise his head and immediately wished he hadn't. Pain stabbed into his temples and bright lights danced and spun across his vision like a tiny meteor shower.

"What the hell is the Scorching? No, wait, don't answer that, yet. We need to get you to the medical bay. Cas said it could fix you up. Then you can explain what's going on with you, your eyes, and all of this." She gestured around them.

"Cas spoke to you?" His ship's AI rarely spoke to anyone but him. For a computer program, it was decidedly picky about who it communicated with.

"It did. It wouldn't give me a damage report, but it did tell me you weren't dying and that the ship wasn't about to blow up."

"Cas, report."

Cas answered in Pyrosian. "Your companion does not take direction well. I informed her you needed to get to the medical bay."

"Keep your opinion to yourself and give me a damage report." Vadir continued to speak in English so that Lisa could understand what he was saying.

"Then will you get yourself to medical?"

"Cas!" he barked and winced as the bellow triggered another wave of pain.

"I can repair everything that is damaged, including you. It will, however, take some time. My power conduits are damaged. Propulsion is inoperative. Communications and signal relay systems are down. There is structural damage to the hull. I have rerouted power to the shields, which should be sufficient to keep us from being detected, however, while we are hidden, it will be impossible for the *Firebrand* to locate us."

"Wonderful," he muttered. "Cas, continue repairs. Prioritize communications. I need to tell Commander Denza what's happened."

"You can tell me who is Commander Denza is on the way to medical." Lisa eased her hand away from his brow and then sighed. "That's not fully clotted yet. Try not to reopen it when you stand up."

"You're taking this all very well." He eased himself into a sitting position and tried to ignore the grinding pain that flared every time he moved.

Lisa got to her knees and moved in closer. She wrapped a steadying arm around his shoulders and then laughed. "Which part? The fact you're bleeding, that you're an alien, or the bit where you kidnapped me, and I ended up sticking around to help you anyway?"

"All of it." he gave in to the need tearing through him and turned his head, capturing her mouth with his. She tensed, and for a second he thought she might push him away again, but then she uttered a soft moan and kissed him back. The fire he'd been fighting to control became an inferno, burning away everything but the need to have her.

Their mouths crashed together in a heated claiming that branded it onto his soul. This was the female he'd been destined for, and he wanted her like he had never wanted another.

Until this moment, he hadn't wanted *this*. The life-long bond forming between them was something he'd hoped to never find. But the Gods, as usual, had ignored his plans.

He kissed her again, savoring the sweet taste of her lips. He could get lost in her body for a month at least, learning every pleasurable curve and line.

"Vee, we should stop. You need to get fixed up."

"No." His response was more growl than an actual word, a sure sign the Scorching was taking over. It wouldn't be long before he would be a slave to the need to claim her, and judging by her ardent response, the Scorching was affecting her, too. That thought gave him the strength to stop. He had to tell her what was to come before it was too late.

He tore his lips from hers with a frustrated curse. "We're running out of time."

"You keep saying that, but you don't explain what happens when our time's up. What happens then? Oh, shit. Is this going to be like one of those movies where the heroine finds an alien, and she has to go on the run to keep him safe from government scientists?"

Part of his short but intense education into Earth's cultures included viewing a number of films and television programs. They were an imaginative species. It was a shame they were as destructive as they were creative. "I've seen those films. They don't make any sense. If a species has the technology to cross the galaxy, wouldn't it make sense they can hide from your primitive detection devices? We're safe from discovery. There's no need to leave the ship."

"Fair point, but now is not the time to get into a conversation about plot holes and creative licence. I'm not too sure I agree with your assessment about being safe, though. You're the one who kidnapped me, remember?"

"I remember. Then you slugged me, and we crashed. I'd say we're almost even."

He got to his feet, which wasn't easy considering the ship was listing to one side. "Cas, why are we sitting at this angle? And respond in English while Lisa is onboard."

"You told me to prioritize repairs on communications."

"I spent half a billion galactic cred on you, and you

can't multitask? I'll get to medical a lot faster if you level the flaming ship."

A shudder passed through the ship, and it began to right itself, finally stopping when the floor was level again.

"Much better."

Lisa had flattened herself against the nearest wall when the ship started to move and didn't move or speak until it was quiet again.

"You still haven't told me why we're running out of time.

"It's the Scorching." He started to make his way down the corridor, and Lisa appeared at his side, slipping an arm around his waist and holding him steady. He ached all over, but it was his head that was going to kill him. Stabbing pain accompanied each step, and the dizziness and nausea made it difficult to walk.

"You keep using that word. What does it mean?"

"It means that you and I were destined for each other. The first time you touched me, there was a Spark. That heralded the beginning of what my people call the Scorching. A mating fever consumes both mates. We're in the thrall of it, now, and it's only going to get stronger."

Lisa froze. "What if I don't want this? I agreed to go out to dinner, not this."

"I never expected this, either. You're not Pyrosian. This shouldn't be possible." He turned to brush a light kiss to the crown of her head. "There's no stopping this, *tani*. At least, not if you feel what I am."

"You mean the flashes of heat and the fact I don't want to leave your side?"

"And the need. Flames and fury, I need you so badly it hurts more than my head does."

She tensed. "Promise me you didn't do this. Swear to me on whatever you hold dear that you didn't give me something or pull some weird alien mind trick to make me agree to fly away with you. "

The edge of fear in her voice cut him deeply. His mate was afraid, and it was his fault. He spoke from his heart and hoped that it would be enough. "I swear on the graves of my parents that I did not do this to you. My people believe it's the Gods that select the perfect match for each of us and reveal them to us when the time is right."

"And what do you believe?"

Vadir felt like he was standing at the edge of a cliff, and the ground was crumbling beneath his feet. He had stopped trusting the Gods the day his father had chosen to follow his mate into death instead of staying to raise his young son. He'd been on his own since then, making his own choices and building a life for himself with no help from anyone. At least, that's what he'd chosen to believe until now.

Staring into Lisa's lovely face, he couldn't deny the truth. "I believe that we are supposed to be together.

That our meeting was the will of the Gods. It has to be. How else can any of this be possible?"

"The will of the Gods, huh?" She drew in a slow breath and then kissed his cheek. "They showed me what you looked like months ago. So I guess I'm going to have to trust them—and you."

"They showed you?"

She started forward again. The medical bay was only six meters away now, and he pointed out the location to her as she continued to explain.

"I was inspired one day and started to sketch a face. Yours."

On his world, only a rare few were gifted with communications from the Gods. Only female Pyrosians manifested the ability, and with the slow decline of female births, many of the bloodlines that carried the gift had been lost.

"I even made your eyes gold, which I didn't understand at the time. That's part of this Scorching thing, too, right?"

"After we have consummated our mating, my eyes will be that colour forever. At least, I think they will. It would indicate that my full powers have been unlocked, but I have no idea if that will happen. I think its likely, though."

He waved his hand over a door panel and a doorway opened in the wall. Inside was an advanced medical bay. Given the amount of time he travelled alone, it had been a good investment, though one he had hoped to never need to use.

"Cas, where do you want your patient?" Lisa asked in a take-charge tone that made his cock surge to attention. He'd spent his life thinking he liked quiet, docile females, so why did her confidence turn him on so much?

"What are you laughing about?" she asked as she helped him onto the bed.

"I was just thinking that it took getting punched by a female from another planet for me to understand what I really wanted. Apparently, I'm as thick-skulled as my critics have always claimed."

"If that's true, then we are going to have some spectacular arguments, Vee. Even my friends say I'm stubborn." She smoothed his hair with a gentle hand and frowned. "I can't believe I'm already talking about a future with you. This Scorching thing is powerful. It's messing with my head. How long does this last?"

"About two of your solar-cycles."

"Two days? What are we going to do for two days? Sit in this broken ship and wait for your buddy Kash to rescue us?"

"No, *tani*. Once Cas has healed my injuries, I am going to take you to my quarters and spend the next two cycles making love to you."

Desire kindled in her eyes. "You're making big promises for a man in a hospital bed."

"I won't be here for long."

"In that case, I should leave so that Cas can get started."

"I don't want you to go." He took her hand and interlocked their fingers. "Stay with me, please."

Her answering smile was brighter than any star in the cosmos. "I'll stay because you asked me to instead of making it a demand. Try doing that more often. You'll be amazed how well it works."

"I'm not used to asking for things, so." He grinned and tugged at her hand. "I'd better start practicing. Would you please kiss me?"

She laughed and leaned over him, her hair spilling across his chest and throat as she kissed him for the first time. "See how well that works?"

6

———

Lisa had expected a gleaming, high tech medical bay stuffed full of wondrous gizmos and gadgets. Instead, the room was so nondescript she would have never guessed its purpose. The walls were a soothing shade of pale blue, and there was a simple counter with what looked like a sink near the head of the bed. That was it.

It wasn't until Vadir lay down that anything interesting happened. A nimbus of golden light appeared around the bed and quickly filled with streams of data as the patient was scanned and assessed. Cas made his diagnosis in Pyrosian, but Vadir translated the gist for her. He had a concussion, contusions, and what he called some 'minor internal damage.'

She kept waiting for robotic arms to appear and start working on Vadir's injuries, but instead, the field around him glowed brighter, and the streams of data started to scroll by faster. As she watched, the cut on his head slowly closed over and began to heal. She should have been fascinated by all she was witnessing, but her focus was all on Vadir. She still had his hand in hers, and every time either one of them shifted so much as a finger, an erotic current flowed through her.

Adding to her distraction, Cas had made Vadir's shirt vanish, and judging by the way Vee had cursed about it, she assumed it had been destroyed in the process. Seeing him half naked was making it almost impossible to focus on what was happening. All she wanted to do was to explore his body and commit every inch of it to memory. Her skin had become so sensitive that even the soft cloth of her dress was an irritant. She couldn't keep a thought in her head for more than two seconds before she'd be back to thinking about Vadir and all the things she wanted to do with him.

"Hurry this up, Cas," Vadir said through gritted teeth.

"Your recovery would be expedited if your blood pressure was lower and your heart rate was slowed by twenty percent."

"That is not going to happen. Do what you can and let me up."

"Wait. You can't move right now?" Lisa asked.

"No. There's a force field holding me in place. Cas

is making sure I stay still until I'm finished treatment." Vadir sounded entirely unimpressed.

"Cas. Can I touch Vadir? I mean, is it safe for me to reach into this glowing field?"

"You are already touching Vadir." The computer pointed out, and a pulse of light flared around their joined hands. "If you move further into the field, I will be able to treat you, as well. You have minor bruising and contusions that I can heal."

"So, that's a yes." Lisa stepped into the field and placed her free hand in the center of Vadir's broad chest. His skin was hot under her fingers, and she could feel his heartbeat racing against his ribs.

"What are you doing? And why didn't you tell me you were hurt?" he demanded.

"I'm distracting you. And I'm just a little bruised, mostly from the harness. You risked your life to make sure I was secured. I won't forget that." Nor would she ever forget the look on his face in the second before impact. He'd put her life ahead of his own, risking everything to protect her as best he could. There were only two other people in the universe who might have done that for her, and they were her closest friends.

She let her fingertips wander over his bare skin, following the lines of muscle down to his sculpted abs. She had expected to feel something from the field, but all she sensed was slight warmth and a sense of wellness that defied description.

"I did what I had to, to keep you safe." He raised his head a fraction to watch as her fingers moved lower. You're playing with fire, *tani*."

"No, I'm playing with you. And what does *tani*, mean?"

"It means you are my treasure. It's a term of endearment in my language."

She moved her hand further down his body, and he groaned. "I should tell you. Once we've mated. You..." his words trailed off as she reached his navel and circled it with her fingertip.

"I'll what?"

"You *will* be playing with fire. The powers I spoke of before. I will be able to summon flames."

"You're joking. Please, tell me you're kidding. I'm coping with the fact you're an alien, and we're on a spaceship. I might even be accepting the fact that we're supposed to be together, considering I can't keep my hands off of you and I...I ache." The confession slipped out before she could stop herself.

"I'm serious." His hand tightened around hers. "There's more I need to tell you, but we're out of time."

"Cas isn't finished yet."

"Finished or not, I can't wait any longer." Vadir's eyes glowed like molten gold as he turned to look at her and spoke a few words in his language.

The nimbus of light faded away, Vadir sat up, and the next thing she knew she was in his arms, his mouth slanted across hers. Hunger tore through her, fueled by needs and desires too powerful to fight. She parted her lips, inviting him to take the kiss deeper. He uttered a low groan that rolled up from his chest and drove his tongue into her mouth.

There was a sharp tearing noise as he tore her dress down the back, the fabric parting like tissue paper.

She shrugged out of the tattered remains and let it fall to her feet. "I thought we were going to your quarters for this part."

He kissed her again, sucking her lower lip into his mouth before finally lifting his head to answer. "That plan went out the airlock once you put your hands on me, mate. I need to have you. Here. Now."

The buttoned up, in control, corporate suit she'd met for dinner tonight was gone, replaced by a cocky, charming, rogue who made her hotter than any man she'd ever been with. The next step was easy. Her choice was already made.

"Then take me before I remember all the reasons I should be running away from you."

He tangled his hand into her hair and tugged her head up so that she was staring into his eyes. "I will make sure you never have reason to run from me again. You're mine, Lisa. From now until we return to the Flame that birthed us. I swear by the Flames of the

First one that I will protect you with my dying breath and cherish you above all others."

"There better not be *any* others, Vee. If we have any chance of being real, then you have to promise me two things. You won't cheat on me, and you'll never hurt me."

"After tonight, no other female in the universe will interest me. I will never cheat on you." He kissed her again, tenderly this time. "And I swear that I will never hurt you. I'm not a barbarian."

She laughed. "Says the man who abducted me before we even got through our first date. You have to admit, that's a little barbaric."

———

Her teasing laughter pushed him to the edge of his control and then blew right past it at light speed. The time for talking was over.

He rose from the bed and drew her into his arms, stripping away the last of her clothing as his mouth plundered hers. *Finally.*

Dressed, she was beautiful. Naked and in his arms, she was breathtaking. Later, he'd take the time to enjoy the view she offered, but for now, he needed her too much to take his time.

Torn between getting out of his pants quickly or

letting go of Lisa, he struggled one-handed until she reached between them to help.

"You don't have to do everything on your own, you know." She eased his pants over his hips and down his thighs, letting her hands stroke over his skin as she did it.

"That's going to take a little getting used to."

He toed off his shoes and kicked away the last of his clothes, placed his hands on her hips, and turned her so that she was facing the bed. "Hands on the bed, *tani*, and don't move."

"The bed is not where I want my hands to be right now."

He moved in behind her, letting his aching cock rest in the cleft of her ass cheeks as he guided her into the position he had in mind. Legs spread, leaning forward, her breasts hanging free and her hair spilling over her shoulders.

"You are stunning," he whispered in her ear.

"And you're talking too much. I feel like I'm losing my mind right now. Make it stop."

"I can't make it stop, but I can make it better. For both of us."

He dropped to his knees and moved between her legs, kissing each soft globe of her ass before lowering himself so he could see the folds of her pussy. She rose up onto her toes as he reached to part her labia and expose the swollen bundle of nerves hidden within. She was already slick with need, her soft skin glistening with the evidence of her arousal. He sucked in a breath, drawing the sweet scent of her deep into his lungs. He blew a puff of air over her skin, and she gasped in surprised pleasure. It was a sound he intended to hear her make over and over again.

Burying his face deep into her pussy, he used his tongue and fingers to tease her honey-slick flesh. She shivered and ground herself against him, uttering a low, breathless moan that made his cock harden to the point of pain. She spread her legs wider, rocking her pussy against his mouth. He drew her clit deeper and lashed it with his tongue as he slid two fingers into her channel and started pumping them in and out in time to the flicking of his tongue.

"Yes," she moaned. "Just like that."

He scissored his fingers, and her inner walls tightened around him as she uttered another wordless moan. Her breaths were coming faster now, and he knew she was close to release. Speeding up the tempo of his assault, he curved his fingers slightly so he could reach the spot his research on female human anatomy indicated would give her the most pleasure.

She came almost immediately, her body quaking as she clamped down on his fingers and ground her pussy hard against his lips, the sweet cream of her arousal flowing over his chin.

Legs trembling, she finally slumped against the

edge of the bed. He rose to his feet, leaning over to plant an open-mouthed kiss to one shoulder blade.

"Whatever challenges we're going to have, I'd say sexual chemistry is not going to be one of them."

He chuckled. "Definitely not."

Lisa's pulse was still thundering in her ears when she glanced back to look at her lover. Vadir was staring at her like she was cherry at the top of his sundae. There was naked hunger in his gaze and a predatory smile on his lips as he rubbed the impressive length of his cock against her ass. His hands landed on her hips, and before she knew it, he spun her around and lifted her into the air. She landed on the bed he'd recently vacated, his hands coaxing her to lie down as his lips claimed hers for another delicious, toe-curling kiss.

"I don't need a check-up. I need you."

"And me is exactly what you're going to get." He walked around to the foot of the bed, running his hands from her bare feet to her ankles.

"As much as I like these, I think they need to go." He unfastened the clasp of her anklet and set it aside, then gripped her legs firmly and tugged her down the bed until her legs were dangling over the edge and her ass was on the edge.

She lifted her head to watch as he fisted his cock in

one hand and moved between her thighs. She was half out of her mind with need already, so when he rubbed the thick head of his cock along the seam of her pussy, she arched her back and nodded in a silent plea.

He eased himself inside, her body giving way to his an inch at a time until there was no room between them. Vadir groaned, his cock throbbing as he muttered in his own language. When he looked up at her, his eyes were flickering gold again, and she knew he was at the edge of his control.

With a grin she arched her hips, managing to slide him a bare fraction of an inch inside. "Move."

His control snapped, and he thrust into her with a guttural groan. "You better hang on."

She gripped the edges of the bed as he settled his hands on her hips and began to move. He stroked her hard and deep for several thrusts, then ground his body against hers so tightly that his balls brushed against her ass and her clit was pressed against his pubic bone. Again and again, he did this, until both of them were sweat-slicked and panting. She was riding a wave of pleasure that lifted her so high she felt as if she were flying.

Vadir was a man possessed by passion, and soon her every nerve flared hotter than the sun as a second climax began to blossom. He reached between her legs and pressed a finger against her clit, sending her spiralling into orgasm as his cock began to thicken and pulse. He came hard, calling out her name as he emptied himself inside her. Instead of softening, his dick continued to swell, pressing against her g-spot and prolonging her own orgasm.

He was slumped over her, one arm bearing most of his weight as he rested his head against her stomach. Both of them fought for breath, and it was a long moment before she had the strength to speak. Gently flexing her inner walls around his still rock-hard cock, she asked, "Is there something else you forgot to mention?"

"I'd forgotten about this, myself. We only reach complete climax with our true mates. This…" He lifted his head to regard her with eyes that had turned to a brilliant gold. "This is something new for me, too."

"Only with me, huh? I like the sound of that."

His lips curved into a sinfully sexy grin. "Only with you. Forever."

"Now, you look like the drawing I made of you. Golden eyes and all." This was the image she'd seen in her mind's eye months ago. She had captured his face at this moment, right down to his arrogant smile.

"And you look…" he trailed off as he stared at her. "By the Flames of the First One, your eyes changed, too."

"What? Changed how? What colour?" She started to sit up, then froze when she realized they were still locked together.

"They're even more lovely now."

"Not helpful. The artist wants words. Details. Tell me exactly what's changed."

"They're the same shade of blue as before, but they glow with an inner fire." He touched his face. "Like I imagine mine do. Now, all who see you will know you are mated. Untouchable. Mine."

"Your eyes are incredible. Just like the rest of you. Are all the men of your species drop-dead gorgeous like you, or do I owe your gods a thank you present for sending me their best?"

"If I answer that honestly, you're going to think I'm an arrogant ass."

"You are arrogant. Or did you think I didn't notice? Your ass, however, is very nice." She bucked her hips lightly. "So, how long are we stuck together like this?"

"Impatient to be free of me already?"

"Not really, no. But I am hungry, and I'm pretty sure there aren't enough cookies in my purse to feed us both. Not if this Scorching thing goes on for days."

He kissed her for a long, heart-stopping moment, and when he finally raised his head, she could feel they were no longer locked together. As he gently withdrew from her, he continued their conversation as if it had never been interrupted. "The mating fever varies slightly from couple to couple, but in general, it lasts two solar cycles. And we don't have much time before we'll need to be together again. Dare I ask why you brought cookies to a dinner date?"

She grinned at him. "Because my roommate thought they'd make a good snack if things went well. Shit. Gwen. She's going to be worried when I don't come home tonight. I didn't send her a text letting her know what I was up to."

"You don't live alone?" Vadir was frowning now.

"My two best friends and I share a house. It's divided up into suites, so we have our privacy, but we watch out for each other. I'm not the only one out on a date tonight, either. I hope Maggie is okay." She froze as her thoughts piled into each other like trucks on an icy freeway.

"Shit! Double shit damn it, how could I forget about Maggie!" She sat up and poked her finger into Vadir's chest. "She's on the same dating site I am. Well, we are. Star-crossed. That one. Please tell me not every guy on there is an alien because she is not going to take that well. Not at all."

"Your friend has been matched on the same dating site as we were?"

Vadir looked shell-shocked. Not a good sign.

"Uh huh. Judging by the expression on your face, I'd guess her match isn't human, either. I need to call her." Lisa looked around for her purse, then swore again. Her phone was in her purse. She must have lost it both during the fight with Vadir, because she couldn't recall having it on her when she came to after the crash.

"I'm afraid you cannot contact your friend," Cas said.

"You don't get to tell me what I can and cannot do. You don't even have opposable thumbs. How are you going to stop me?"

"It is not necessary to stop you. Your phone will not work. We impacted in an area outside the area serviced by your cellar device."

Damn it. Maggie was on her own. "If she meets with this guy, he won't hurt her, right?"

Vadir stood and offered her his hand. "Come with me. I'll explain, but not here. We don't have long before the Scorching will flare again, and there's more I need to tell you. If your friend has been matched to Joran, then I can assure you, he won't harm her. He is the next king of Pyros, and a man of honour."

"He's the *what*?" She hopped off the bed, took his hand, then glanced down at her clothes. They were torn and unwearable. "You owe me dinner, something to wear, and a whole bunch of explanations."

"He's the Crown Prince of my planet, and a friend. Since we were the only two with matches in this part of the world, it's safe to assume your friend is his mate. This is concerning since every effort was made to ensure that none of our matches had close relationships. It would make it difficult for them to leave undetected."

Vadir led her out of the medical bay and down the corridor. She noted that there was more light now. Cas' repairs were progressing.

"You keep talking about me leaving. This is my home, Vadir! I can't just run off with you, no matter how hot the sex is."

"I can't stay here for long without being detected. It's not safe for me to remain. I'm here because my people are dying out. You, and others like you, are our last hope. If you come with me, you will be treated like a queen. You will want for nothing. I swear it. You and our children will be cherished by all."

He passed his hand over another panel, and a portion of the wall vanished, forming a doorway. Beyond, was the most luxurious room she'd ever seen.

The walls were deep blue and mottled with subtle patterns that moved in a hypnotic flow across the surface. The furnishings were elegant and more ornate than anything else she'd seen on board. Polished wood carved with intricate designs, rich fabrics in varying shades of white and cream. There was a work space in one corner, with monitors and what looked like a highly stylised version of a keyboard, but most of the room was taken up by a large circular bed covered in a satiny looking coverlet of midnight blue.

One look at the bed and her head was full of erotic

visions of her and Vadir in the middle of that soft expanse, sweat-slicked, limbs entangled and panting with need. The flames of desire rekindled in a rush, and she turned to Vadir, only to find him striding towards her with his eyes gleaming and his cock already hard and ready.

Whatever else he had to tell her, it would have to wait. The only thing she wanted right now, was him.

7

It had taken a long, glorious soak in Vadir's bathtub to banish the worst of the aches and stiffness from Lisa's body. Two days of marathon sex had left her feeling deliciously used and abused in all the right spots.

The time alone had given her a much-needed chance to ponder everything she'd learned over the last few days. The Scorching had fogged her mind for much of the time, but Vadir had answered all her questions, clarifying things until she finally understood the basic issues. Pyros had a population problem. It had started as a minor dip in the number of girls being born, but instead of self-correcting, the anomaly had increased with each new generation.

Now, there were seven men to every woman born on the planet, and their population was dwindling rapidly. Vadir's species could only reproduce with their true mate. So far, there was only one exception to this rule. Humans. To the Pyrosians, it was a miracle that there was another species they could interbreed with. No one had expected the pairings to be true matches. They hadn't been prepared for either the Spark or the Scorching. Reports would have to be made, and future expeditions would take that into consideration.

Future expeditions. She didn't like the way that sounded. Now that she was thinking clearly, she had more questions for Vadir. A lot more. And a small, worried voice whispered to her that no matter how amazing the last few days had been, she might not like his answers, or what came next.

She rose from the water and towelled off, still organizing her thoughts. She could hear Vadir speaking indistinctly from the other room. He must be talking to Cas, though the only voice she could hear was his. By the time she was dry and had the knots combed out of her hair, she could hear him clearly, loud enough to pull her out of her musings and focus on what he was saying.

"I'm going to need to buy a different house when we get home. Something airy and light, with a studio for Lisa. In the capital would be best, then she can still see her friend whenever she wishes."

She listened to him mutter to himself and wondered if she should make a noise to let him know she could hear him.

"Yes, that'll work. That way when I'm gone, she won't be lonely. If our children have her gifts, they'll need training. Protection. Flames, so will she."

Gifts? What gifts? And what did he mean when he said he'd be gone? She stomped back into his bedroom, intent on asking him what he meant, but there was no one there. "Vadir?" She called, despite the fact she could see the room was empty.

"I need to talk to Joran once communications are back up. Confirm he claimed his mate. Then let Kash know there's a problem with the roommate. How did that get missed? If this were my operation, the entire research department would be fired. Too many details got overlooked. It's sloppy."

She could still hear him clearly. As if he were standing only a few feet away. She spun around, confused and a little alarmed.

"Cas, where's Vadir?"

"He is currently in the engine room, facilitating repairs."

"Where's the engine room?"

"Lower deck, forward compartment. Do you wish to join him?"

Hell, yes, she wished to join him. Maybe he could explain why she could hear him even though he was on the far end of the ship. "Yes."

"Follow the orange lights. I will guide you there."

Lisa grabbed the shirt Vadir had left out for her,

pulling it on as she headed for the door. Vadir had taught her how to activate the doorways and instructed Cas to give her free range of the ship.

Once out in the corridor, she followed the series of strobing, orange lights that Cas used like electronic breadcrumbs to show her the way. She could still hear Vadir, but it slowly dawned on her as she walked that she could hear him better when she concentrated on what he was saying...or thinking. It was obvious that she wasn't really hearing him at all. Was this something else Vadir had forgotten to mention? Would he know what was going on or react with unease when he found out what she could do?

She stepped out of the lift and turned left without even looking at the guide lights. Now that they were on the same level, she could feel his presence and walked towards him with total surety. He was still musing to himself, but his focus seemed to be on repairing a power coupling. At least, that's the little she understood. Apparently, she didn't need to speak his language to understand his basic thoughts, but technical jargon was beyond her.

The air down here was stale and warm. The narrow passageway walls were barely far enough apart to let her walk through without side-stepping, and the ceiling was lined with an array of pipes and conduits that stretched the length of the ship.

"Vee?"

Vadir's head popped out a door at the end of the corridor. "Hi. Cas and I have almost finished repairing communications. The broadcasting array on the hull was wrecked in the crash, and it took longer than expected. I didn't intend to leave you alone so long."

"I was fine with being on my own for a while. We've been in each others' constant company for the past two days. I've never experienced anything that...intense."

"Me, either." He came out to join her, eyeing her with open appreciation. "You look better in that shirt than I ever did. I see you didn't bother with the footwear I found for you. Is there a reason for that?"

"I like being barefoot. But that wasn't the real reason. I was in a hurry to see you. Something weird happened." She touched her temple. "I could hear you. I thought you'd come back, but there wasn't anyone in the room. It took me some time to realize it wasn't your voice I was hearing. It was your thoughts."

He stared at her. "You read my mind? Are you certain? What was I thinking?"

"You weren't impressed that no one had noticed I had roommates, and that if they worked for you, you'd fire the entire research team. And you were thinking about buying a house, one with a studio because I'd need something to do while you were gone."

She folded her arms across her chest. "And we're going to talk about *that* issue once we deal with the fact I woke up telepathic."

"We can't test my theory since there's no one else around, but I suspect the only mind you can read, is mine. I told you that true mates form a bond between them." He touched his chest, then reached out to tap a finger over her heart. "Ours is stronger than most. Likely because you are psychically gifted."

"Does this mean you can read my mind, too?" She wasn't sure how she felt about any of this, but if she could sense Vadir's thoughts, it seemed only fair he could read hers.

"I don't know." He gave her a perplexed look. "How would I even try?"

"I was thinking about you when it started. So, try focusing on me."

Vadir's lips curved into a sexy grin that made her clit throb and her breath catch in her throat.

"I think I can manage that."

"Let's start with something simple. I'll think of a word, and you tell me if you hear it in your head. Ready?"

He nodded, and she tried to stay focused on a single word.

A split second later, Vadir's eyes widened, and his mouth fell open in shock. "Alien. I heard you, even though I was watching your mouth and you never said a word. This is the strongest version of the bond. No matter how far apart we are, we'll always be able to connect with each other."

"You mean all those times you plan on leaving me alone, I will still sense your thoughts?" She didn't mean for the words to come out quite so acidic.

"We haven't had time to discuss that, yet. We still need to negotiate terms and work out a deal so that both of us are happy."

She didn't like his cool tone or the even colder words he was using. "This isn't a deal you're brokering, Vee. This is my life. I understand that you can't stay here. It's too dangerous for you to do that. But I'm not about to follow you across the galaxy to live in a strange world if you don't even plan on being there with me. At the very least, can't I come back home to Earth when you go away?"

"No, you can't. That's one of the things we need to talk about." He ran a hand through his hair, frustration pouring off of him in waves.

"What do you mean, I can't come back?"

"We're not supposed to be in this part of the galaxy at all. And there are rules against making contact with races before they've reached certain milestones. Your race isn't ready. We're here in secret to save our race from extinction. In doing so, we might be saving humans, too. You're a primitive, destructive species, and it's more than likely you'll destroy yourselves before long."

"Primitive? You think I'm primitive?" She took a step back as his words slashed a hole in her heart. She knew better than to fall for someone fast. It was a sure fire way to get hurt, but it hadn't stopped her from starting to care about him. Had she made a terrible mistake?

"I think you're an amazing, gifted female who happens to be from a primitive race. But you are also Pyrosian. Your eyes and our bond prove that. That bond is a two-edged sword, though. If something happens to you, the consequences are significant. I have to make sure you're protected at all times so that I never have to face that. I intend to give you everything you could ever want and keep you in the greatest luxury imaginable, but it will be somewhere I know that you'll be safe."

She could hear a whisper of pain threaded through his words, but she was too furious to pay it any heed. She didn't want to. Not after what he'd said. "I'm a person, not a possession. You can't lock me away and expect me to be grateful. I won't live my life that way."

Vadir's eyes were hooded and his brow furrowed into deep lines. "You don't have any choice, *tani*. We're mated. Connected. You said it yourself, this is your destiny. The deal is done, you can't renege now. I promise I will take care of you and give you everything you wish."

"What if I wish to be able to return to Earth? Or explore Pyros, or travel with you to other planets? Then what happens to your promises? What if I don't stay in this gilded cage you've offered me and I go out exploring on my own because you left me alone?"

"Then I will find you and bring you home again," he said, his words clipped and his tone flat and cold.

All the hope and joy she had found in the last few days faded away to despair and heartache. Her father had talked that way. Treating Lisa and her mother like possessions to be jealously protected and confined. His conviction that he owned them had driven him to violence over and over again. Until finally her mother had taken Lisa and fled. There was no way she would ever make the mistake her mother had. She would not stay with a man who saw her as a possession.

"Earth is my home. Until you understand that, we don't have anything more to discuss." She turned her back on him and walked away. His thoughts started to pour into her head, but she shut them out, visualizing a wall so thick and tall that nothing could get through it. She didn't want to know what he was thinking right now, and she didn't want him to catch even a glimmer of what she intended to do next.

That didn't go as planned. Vadir had miscalculated. His head said he needed time to rethink his plan and come up with a new offer, but his heart wanted to go after Lisa and do his best to fix the pain that had flashed in her beautiful eyes as she turned from him. He tried to read her thoughts, or at least get a sense of her emotions, but he couldn't get anything. It was as if she'd sealed herself off. He didn't like the way it felt.

He stayed where he was, watching in silence as she walked back to the lift and vanished through the doors without looking back even once. He knew this move. She'd walked away from the bargaining table, and it was up to him to find a reason for her to come back.

Negotiating tactics were something he could understand. The deal was in freefall, and it was his fault. He'd failed to explain things to her clearly, to make her understand why he needed her safe.

Since meeting Lisa, he had finally started to understand why his father had succumbed to the Fading and followed his mate into the afterlife. The Scorching was more powerful than he had imagined, and the newly formed bond he had to Lisa was already changing his life in a hundred different ways.

He had come to Earth because he'd been ordered to. He hadn't been prepared for any of this. Not the bonding, or the desire, or the need to protect the woman who had become the centre of his world in a matter of days. When they had children, he would do better for them than his father had done for him. They would never have to face the pain of growing up without their mother. He'd see to it.

All he had to do now was to find the right

leverage and finalize things with Lisa. His research had led him to believe that offering her riches would have been enough. Obviously, that wasn't the case. Worse, he was running out of time. Communications would be back up soon, and once a few more parts were delivered from the mother ship in orbit, they'd be leaving. He needed to have Lisa's agreement to come with him to Pyros before that happened.

Whatever it took, he'd give it to her.

He was still no closer to figuring things out when Cas interrupted his train of thought.

"Our passenger has disembarked. Will she not be returning to the *Firebrand* with us for the journey back to Pyros?"

"What? What do you mean she disembarked? I gave you orders not to let her off the ship!"

He dropped the calibrator he'd been working with and scrambled to his feet. His mate had left him. He'd never heard of such a thing. It didn't make any sense. Everyone knew Pyrosians mated for life. Where did she think she could go?

"You also ordered me to allow her free run of the ship and access to all doorways. Did you not intend for that command to include the exits?"

"No, I did not! Are you tracking her right now? Where did she go, Cas?"

"My external sensors indicate she is moving down the mountain we crashed on. At her current rate of descent, she will not reach the bottom before nightfall. I am concerned she may be in danger from the local wildlife. I have detected large predatory carnivores in the area."

"Flames and fury, what is she thinking?" He bolted out of the engine room and made for the airlock on this deck, bouncing off the walls of the narrow passageway more than once along the way.

"I believe she is thinking she is done with arrogant aliens, busted ships, and controlling, possessive assholes. At least, that is what she muttered prior to her departure."

"Not helpful, Cas. When we get back home, remind me to look into giving you an empathy subroutine."

"That might be wise. Perhaps a relationship coun-selling program might also be—"

"Shut up, Cas."

Fear and anger churned in a bitter stew in his stomach as he activated the outer doors and leapt to the ground. They'd crashed into a stretch of grassy meadow, which was the only reason either of them was still breathing. If Cas hadn't managed to restart the engines at the last minute and make a desperate course correction, they'd have hurtled into the thick woods that surrounded them. The impact would have torn the ship, and them, to pieces.

He spotted a flash of bright blue at the bottom end of the meadow and started to run towards it. He knew instinctively it was her, though the colour confirmed it. That was the shirt he'd left out for Lisa this morning. Shirts and a pair of thick socks were the only things he'd left for her because it was all he had that fit. She wasn't dressed for a walk in a cultivated park, never mind a hike through the wilderness.

"Lisa!" He bellowed her name as he pounded through the blend of tall grass and wildflowers, sending petals and seeds flying in all directions.

She turned to look at him, and he stumbled when her voice rang inside his head at full volume. *"Leave me alone!"*

"Never."

He didn't know if she'd get the message or not, so he called out to her as well. "We're bound together for life. I couldn't leave you alone if I tried."

Her bitter laugh floated to him on the breeze. *"Try anyway."*

There was so much pain, and anger tangled up with her thoughts, it made his heart ache. As much as he wanted to run to her, he recognized that wasn't the right thing to do. When he was still fifteen meters away, he slowed to a walk, then came to a stop when they were near enough to talk without having to yell.

She stood and watched his approach, every part of her tensed and ready to bolt despite the fact she was wearing nothing but his shirt. Her hair was bound back in a tight braid, and her glowing eyes were full of wary distrust.

"I don't want to try and leave you. I want to try and understand why you left," he told her.

She snorted with derision. "It shouldn't be that hard to figure out. How would you feel if someone came to you, made you feel special, and then told you that you were now their possession with no rights and no say in your own life?"

"I didn't say that."

"Yes, you did. You couched it in pretty words, but it all means the same thing. You're just like my dad. You think people are things to be owned and controlled. You tried to negotiate a deal with me. You tried to offer me trinkets in exchange for giving up my freedom, my friends, and my *life*."

"I am not like your father. He murdered your mother, correct? I don't wish to hurt you, Lisa. I want to protect you."

"No, you want to control me. That makes you very much like him. You even threatened to hunt me down and bring me back if I left you."

"I don't want to control you. I..." He gave a frustrated snarl and threw his hands out as the truth exploded out of him. "I don't know what I want. I never expected to find my mate, and now here you are. Vulnerable. Beautiful. You hold my heart, and my life, in your hands and you don't even know it, yet."

"What are you talking about? I slugged you once and crashed your damned ship. How vulnerable can I be?"

He didn't want to talk about this. Didn't want to revisit the dark memories he kept so carefully buried, but it was the only way she would understand why he needed to protect her. Reluctantly, he sank down into the sweet-smelling grass and gestured for her to join him.

"You've told me about your parents. I think it's time I told you about mine."

8

—————

Walking away wasn't a good plan. She'd known that when she'd set out, but she needed to put some distance between her and Vadir. Two days of being confined to the ship hadn't helped with her mood, either. She needed to breathe fresh air and feel the sun on her face. Or rain. At this point, she'd go for a walk in a thunderstorm and risk being struck by lightning rather than stay put a second longer.

Outside, the weather was idyllic. Only a few puffy white clouds were scattered across the wide expanse of blue sky, and a warm summer breeze waltzed through the tall grass, making the golden heads dance and bob. The ship had crashed near the centre of the meadow, leaving deep furrows in the ground where it had first hit before sliding to a stop some fifty metres later.

She'd been able to see the ship at first, but once she walked a few feet away, whatever shielding technology Cas was using kicked in. The next time she'd looked back, the entire vessel had vanished.

Neat trick, and it certainly explained why no one had noticed them.

She had barely started thinking things through when Vadir's shout shattered the peace, and now she was face to face with him again, still hurting and raw from what he'd said to her. She didn't want to talk to him, but it was evident from the speed he'd come after her that he wasn't giving her a choice.

Once he was seated, she did the same, stretching out her bare legs in front of her. "if you really wanted to convince me you weren't trying to control my every move, you might have considered waiting ten minutes before charging after me, bellowing my name."

"Cas told me you left the ship and appeared to be heading towards the base of the mountain. I took off after you after I was informed there were large carnivores in the area. What were you going to do if you came across one, throw my socks at them and make a run for it barefoot?"

"I wasn't going to try and hike out of here on foot. I'm not that crazy. I needed to get outside and think in peace. Not that you let that happen."

"And the carnivores don't concern you?"

"Bears and cougars are not likely to attack me in the middle of a meadow. I know better than to get between a bear and her cubs, or their kill. If Cas detected that much wildlife in the area, we must have travelled further than I thought.

"According to Cas, we're on somewhere on the eastern slope of one of the mountains in the Garibaldi Range. We won't know our exact coordinates until a few more repairs are completed, but it won't be long, now." He sat back and looked around them. "You're certain we're safe out here?"

"I'm sure. You don't spend much time outdoors, do you?"

A shadow darkened his eyes. "I used to. When I was a youngling, we spent a lot of time outside. Hiking. Swimming. Exploring the woodland outside the city where we lived."

"What happened?" She wasn't even sure why she asked the question. They had other things to talk about, but something told her this was important.

"My mother died. She drowned while swimming in the lake she'd been visiting every year since before I was born. A storm blew in, and she was too far away from shore to make it back. My dad took a boat out and tried to reach her, but he didn't make it in time."

"I'm sorry, Vee. I know what it's like to lose a parent."

"That's the part I need to explain to you, *tani*. I didn't lose one parent. I lost them both." He broke off a long stem of grass and began stripping away the leaves as he spoke. "Among my people, the bond between mates doesn't end with death. The survivor suffers what we call the Fade. It's the desire to escape this life and join their beloved in the next world. Just as the bond between mates varies from couple to couple, so does the strength of the Fade. For some, it's little more than a whisper. For others, it's a pull too powerful to resist."

Lisa's heart twisted in her chest. "Your father? He Faded?"

Vadir lifted his head, and she could see the answer to her question in his eyes. They were haunted and full of grief. "He died less than a year after her death. I never understood how he could do that to me. Not until you came along."

"Don't tell me you'd die for me, Vadir. You don't know me well enough to even think along those lines. We're almost strangers. A few days of mind melting sex doesn't mean we're in love with each other."

He shook his head and tossed the mangled grass aside. "We're so much more than that. You're my *mate*, Lisa. My true match. The only woman in the world I will ever desire. The Scorching is more than a mating fever. It's the moment when two souls are forged together. It's been two days, and you can already read my thoughts. Imagine what this will be like in a month, or a year. If something happens to you, I'll make the same choice my father did."

"You don't get to put that on me, Vadir. We're all responsible for our own actions. You came here. You contacted me. You caused all of this. Now you have to own it."

He started to argue, but then the fire went out of his eyes, and he dropped his hands to his sides. "I don't know how to do this."

It was probably the only thing he could have said that wouldn't push her further away. "You don't know how to do what?"

"Trust other people. I stopped doing that a long time ago."

She remembered how that felt. She learned from her mother that it was best not to trust anyone else, and easier to rely on only what she could do for herself. That way, no one could disappoint or betray you. Gwen was the first person, beside her mom, that Lisa learned she could rely on. Later, Maggie had proven herself, too. Without them, Lisa knew her life would be very different, and a lot lonelier.

"If we have any chance of making this work, you're going to have to trust me. You can't control my life or my choices."

"But I need—"

She cut him off. "You need. You want. Your life. Do you see the pattern here? This isn't a negotiation at all. You're dictating the terms of my prison sentence, and expecting me to agree." She glared at him and huffed in frustration. "And now you have me talking like this was a business deal and not a relationship."

"Deals are simple. You negotiate for what you want, sign a contract, and live up to your promises. You, are not simple, Lisa Woods. You're complicated and messy."

She laughed. "You forgot sexy and wildly unpredictable. And I'd like to point out that for the last two days you've been just as hedonistic and crazy as I have. Not to mention the fact you literally set our bed on fire."

He broke off another piece of grass and stared at it until it smoked, then burst into flame. He let it burn almost to his fingers before banishing the flame with a wave of his hand. "That was the Scorching. Normally I have more control than that."

"Control is your problem, Vee. Sometimes, you have to let go. Honestly, I think you've got more fire in you than you want to admit. You've held yourself in check for so long, you've forgotten who you were."

A crazy, terrifyingly bad idea struck her. "I want to know what it feels like when you burn. I want to know who you are behind the walls and rules and buttoned up suits." She drew up her legs so that she was sitting cross-legged, then beckoned him over. "I'll show you mine if you show me yours."

Puzzled, he rose to his feet and came to where she sat, taking her hand before sitting down so that he was facing her. "What do you want to show me, *tani*?"

"The truth. Mine and yours. I'm not sure how to do this, but I'm going to try and drop the walls and let you into my head. The Gods put us together and gave us this ability, right? So, we should probably use it."

He crooked a dark brow. "And if we don't like what we find?"

"Then the Gods suck at matchmaking, and we'll know to stop trying to make this work." She tried to sound glib, but the words fell flat. This was a huge risk, and she had no idea if it would work. Hell, there were parts of her own psyche she didn't want to examine too closely. Now she was about to expose herself to Vadir. Scars, regrets, and all.

Vadir had come to Earth prepared to offer his match anything she wanted. Money, jewels, and gifts from across the galaxy. The one thing he hadn't planned on giving her was any part of himself. He gripped her hand and wondered if the Gods were laughing at him right now.

"Ready?" she asked.

"Yes."

There was silence for a long moment as the two of them stared at each other. Birds sang and twittered to each other, the breeze swirled around them, thick with the scent of wild flowers and green, growing things. His attention was caught by a small insect with large, multi-coloured wings that fluttered overhead. That was when it happened. His eyes still saw one view, but inside his head, he saw the same creature from another angle.

"Lisa?"

Warmth and a trace of amusement coloured her reply. *"Yes."*

He closed his eyes and cautiously followed her thoughts back to their source. At the same time, he felt her presence in his mind, a gentle flutter that reminded him of the winged insect he'd been watching.

"Butterfly." She gave him the creature's name.

Thoughts and feelings flowed over him like water from a stream. There were undercurrents of mood, and quicksilver glimpses of memory, but all of it was her. Her strength and empathy, her fire and ferocity. He bore witness to her darkest memories and was amazed by the depth of her bonds to her two dearest friends.

There had been wild choices and a reckless need to push her limits and face her fears. Where he had channelled his anger and pain into forging a future for himself and controlling the world around him, she had gone a different way. She'd leapt off a bridge with nothing but a cord around her ankles and dived naked into fast-flowing rivers. There was a tattoo of a flower hidden in the hair above her left ear. It was a legacy of a youthful bet she carried as a reminder that some choices cannot be undone.

There was a scar on his arm that served the same purpose. He started to understand. They weren't that different. Two lives, lived differently but fuelled by the same fire.

"Now do you see?" Her voice was a gentle whisper in his mind.

"Yes. Do you?" He'd been so entranced by his experience, he'd forgotten that she was learning about him, too. Had she found the answers she sought?

Laughter sounded, soft and sweet. *"Yes. We're more alike than I imagined. Maybe the Gods knew what they were doing, after all."*

"After this, I have no doubts. I was wrong to think I could lock you away and keep you safe that way."

She laughed aloud. "Damn right you were."

He opened his eyes to find her looking at him with affection. "The Gods didn't send me here to retrieve a gentle female to raise my children. They brought me to Earth to present me with my perfect partner."

He tugged at her hand, and she came willingly into his arms. "Come home with me, *tani*."

She twined her arms around his neck and leaned in close enough her breath was a silken caress across his lips. "I want to visit the worlds I saw in your memories."

"Wherever you want to go, I'll take you. "

"No gilded cage?" she whispered.

"No cage at all. And maybe, when we're ready, you and I can find a place that both of us can call home."

"You've got yourself a deal."

He dropped his head to slant a kiss across her smiling lips. *"Finally."*

She didn't answer him in words. Instead, she sent him a vivid image of the two of them making love in the grass; clothes scattered, her hair blowing in the breeze as she knelt over him, his hands on her breasts.

He speared one hand into her hair and wrapped his other one around her waist before letting himself fall backwards, taking her with him.

"Aren't you getting ahead of yourself? We're still dressed."

"Not for long." He tossed his communicator out of range, then conjured a flame with a snap of his fingers. He let it grow into a blazing sphere with the two of them at its center. Their clothes burned away in a flash, and he dispelled the effect with a thought.

She blinked down at him, her dazzling eyes wide

with shock. "Are you insane? You could have set the whole forest burning!"

"My control is better than that, now. I wouldn't risk you or Cas that way. As my mate, you're immune to my fires, but if it spread...I don't know how far that immunity goes, and I don't ever intend to find out."

"I still think you're a lunatic. It's a good thing I like you this way."

"I'm only a lunatic where you're concerned."

She wriggled her hips, grinding herself lightly across his fast hardening cock. "That might be the nicest thing you've ever said to me."

***

Lisa leaned down and brushed her mouth over Vadir's. The Scorching might be over, but her need for him hadn't lessened at all. She left her mind open, letting him read her thoughts as she slid down his body, leaving a trail of kisses down his chest and stomach as she worked her way south.

She teased him with feather-soft caresses and touches, nibbling and kissing his golden skin. The anticipation built with every second that passed. Desire swirled between them, and when she finally grazed her lips across the broad head of his cock, Vadir groaned with eagerness and thrust his hips upwards.

"Suck me."

"Patience," she sent the thought to him before settling herself between his muscular thighs and bowing her head to take him deep into her mouth.

"I prefer immediate gratification."

She laughed without removing her mouth from his shaft, letting the vibration roll through him as she wrapped one hand around his thick base and slipped the other between his legs to cup his sac. Vadir's arousal flowed through their link to intertwine with hers, amplifying the experience until she was drunk with pleasure.

He dug his fingers into the grass beneath them, his breath coming in ragged gasps. "Flames, that feels good. But you know that, don't you? You can feel what I'm feeling."

She uttered a low hum of agreement and swiped her tongue across the slit of his cock while stroking her fingertips over his balls. They tightened, and his cock twitched and swelled in her mouth. He was close. She could sense the slow corkscrewing tangle of desires as his orgasm loomed. She used their connection to push him higher, every bob of her head and stroke of her tongue timed to take him to the brink without going over.

She kept him there until he his every muscle was taut as a bowstring and his thrusts had become broken and uneven. That was the moment she released him and rocked back on her heels, her arms outstretched in open invitation. "I want to know what it feels like when you're inside me. Do you think we can do that? Stay linked?"

He lifted his head and gave her a wicked smile. "Only one way to find out. Come here."

He sat up, his long legs stretched out in front of him, his cock rising from between his thighs to rest against his stomach. He crooked a finger at her, then patted his thighs.

Lisa rose to her feet and stretched luxuriously, deliberately making Vadir wait.

His gaze never wavered, and the hungry expression on his face was enough to make her heart race. No man had ever looked at her the way he did as if she were everything he craved, and all he needed.

She stepped over his torso and then lowered herself onto his lap, letting him guide her down. She straddled him, crouching, his cock pressed along the seam of her pussy as she wrapped her arms around his neck and kissed him. Every move they made resulted in a delicious friction that sent her libido rocketing into overdrive within seconds.

"I need you," he whispered the words into her mouth, one arm curving around her waist to steady her as he reached between them to stroke a finger across her aching clit.

"I'm all yours," she whispered back, and there was

no ignoring the note of truth behind the words. She'd made her choice, and she had no regrets.

"From now until we return to the Flame that birthed us," he murmured, then kissed her hard as he guided his cock to her entrance. His arm tightened around her waist, bringing them together with deliberate slowness.

She didn't want slow. She wanted it hard, and fast, with no rules and no barriers between them. Rocking backward, she leaned against his hold and took him deep, shifting her weight off her legs so that she could wrap them around his hips.

He growled and leaned back, opening the angle between them. His fingers toyed with her clit, rubbing the little nub in tiny circles as he started a bouncing, thrusting motion that drove their bodies together.

His pleasure overlapped her own, the sensations swirling together until she couldn't tell which belonged to whom. Not that she cared. She was lost in a firestorm of desires that consumed everything in its path.

Her position shifted as he drew up his knees and placed his feet on the ground, cradling her body in his as he leaned back and braced himself on one arm. She released her arms from around his neck and leaned back against his thighs, then cried out as the new angle sent his cock plunging over her g-spot. Her inner walls clenched hard, and both of them gasped at the surge of raw sensation that erupted.

The intensity was more than she could take, and she gave in to the inevitable with a shuddering cry. Vadir's control broke seconds later, and they rode out their mutual climaxes with both mind and body intertwined in perfect bliss.

9

———————

Sated and content, Vadir was stretched out on the sun drenched grass with Lisa nestled into his side. Beyond the birdsong and trill of the insects was a deep silence that resonated deep in his heart. For once, his mind was still, and he felt entirely at peace. He looked up into the clear blue sky and felt a pang of regret that they wouldn't be able to return here. Earth had proven to be far more interesting, and beautiful, than he'd expected, despite the disappointment of all the business opportunities he'd been denied.

Beside him, Lisa tensed, then sat up. "Who said you can't do business here? And you still haven't explained why I can't come back here to visit."

Damn it. The telepathic link between them was going to take some getting used to.

"I told you that we're not supposed to have first

contact with any species that haven't met certain developmental criteria. Our being here at all is a violation of some very serious laws."

"You didn't explain. You mentioned it in the middle of a fight, and it hasn't come up again until now. So, explain now, please."

"Remind me to have a learning program developed for the next batch of female mates that are approached so that none of this gets forgotten in future."

She snorted with laughter. "I'll make notes for you, so you don't miss anything important. Now, will you please explain why I can't come home again? And for that matter, how are you going to explain the presence of human women on your planet if you're not supposed to be here?"

"I believe the official cover story will be that you were all found onboard a slaving vessel. At least, that's the last version I heard. The hope was that we would be able to keep your existence a secret for a few years before anyone was the wiser."

"And how exactly am I going to be able to travel around with you if I'm supposed to be a secret?" she asked, looking both amused and mildly annoyed.

"I hadn't figured that out, yet, but I would have come up with a way. I made you a promise. I intend to keep it." He reached up to tap his index finger to the tip of her nose. "Your eyes would make it problematic for you to stay here, too. Your Pyrosian heritage is show-ing, and that puts you at risk."

"There's something else that needs to go on the list. How the fuck did I end up with alien DNA?"

He shrugged and took a moment to find the right words. "We're not sure. We've been a spacefaring race for millennia. There was a time we sent out scores of colony ships. Some failed. Others succeeded. Many stopped communicating and were declared lost. Our best guess is that one of those lost ships landed on your planet, and they discovered that interbreeding was possible."

"So your ancestors got it on with my ancestors, and here I am?"

"It would seem so, yes."

She frowned. "But then why is there so much fuss about first contact? Clearly, that's already happened. My DNA proves it."

He started to answer her before it occurred to him that he had no idea what to say. She was right. It wasn't official, and it certainly wasn't sanctioned, but there had been contact between their species.

"Vee?"

"You're right. By the Flames of the First One, you're absolutely right!" He sat up and kissed her. "Con-vincing the Inter-planetary Council of this won't be easy, but we'll find a way. You know what this means, don't you?"

"It means I might get to visit Spain someday?"

"More than that, *tani*. So much more. If we can bypass the rules, then everything changes. We can approach your governments and begin the process of indoctrinating your species into the council. Better yet, I will be able to negotiate trade agreements. It will be slow at first, but eventually, Earth will have access to technology and knowledge beyond imagining."

"That sounds amazing, and I'm all for it, but...what are we going to trade for it? As you have pointed out more than once, we're a primitive species."

He cupped her face in his hand, his thumb stroking her cheek. "Isn't it obvious? Earth has the one thing we need more than anything else. Single females willing to go to Pyros and be mated."

"If they put you up as a poster boy, I promise, you'll be overwhelmed by volunteers."

"I've already found my mate. We'll choose someone else to be the face of Pyros." He leaned in to kiss her, grateful to the Gods that they had gifted him with a mate who was as intelligent as she was beautiful.

"Mmm good point. You're spoken for."

She was quiet for a second, but he could sense her thoughts and knew she was thinking of her friend, Gwen.

"I want to take my friend with us when we go. Gwen was rejected by the Star-Crossed dating site.

They said she was too old, but she's only two years older than I am! She told me about it before I went out on my date with you. Fuck, she's got to be out of her mind with worry by now. As far as she knows, I went out on a date and vanished."

"As soon as we have communication back, we'll make sure she knows you're alright. As for bringing her with us, that's not my call to make. The *Firebrand* is Joran's ship, and he's the prince, so the final decision is his."

Instead of being distressed, Lisa beamed. "If Joran is with Maggie, then there's no way he'll say no. In fact, I bet she's already got things organized and Gwen's packing right now, and both of them are cursing me out for running late, as usual."

"You've got a good excuse." Vadir jerked his head back towards the crash site.

"Yeah. I slugged you, you fell into the console, activated the emergency engine cutoff thingy, and we crashed." She blushed. "I don't think I've said it, yet. But I really am sorry about that."

"Don't apologize. I deserved that punch. We lived. The ship is nearly repaired, and we had the time we needed to figure things out. As hostile negotiations go, this wasn't so bad."

Lisa was still laughing at him with Cas buzzed his communicator, which was still lying where he tossed it, somewhere in the deep grass. The two of them scrambled around, naked and laughing, until he finally located it and opened a channel.

"Yes, Cas?"

"Repairs to communication and navigation are complete. You should be able to contact Commander Denza and the *Firebrand* whenever you're ready."

"Do you have a list of the parts required to finish repairing the ship before we can fly again?"

"Confirmed. The file is already loaded onto your communicator."

He started to open a channel to the *Firebrand*, then glanced over at Lisa and shut the device off. This conversation would go faster if he were in visual contact, but that wasn't going to happen. Not at the moment.

Lisa's brow creased, and she cocked her head to the left. "Don't you need to talk to the Commander and Joran? The ship needs fixing, we need rescuing, and I want to know how Maggie and Gwen are."

"And I will convey all of that, right after we get dressed." He rose to his feet, then offered her his hand.

"What, you don't want to let your friends see you naked and frolicking in a meadow? Bad for your buttoned-up businessman reputation?" she teased.

He swatted her ass and chuckled before pulling her into his arms. "No, *tani*. I didn't want my companions to see my mate naked. That delight is for me alone."

"If that's the case, then I'm going to need to borrow another one of your shirts."

The vision of her draped in his clothing, legs and feet bare, had his cock surging to life again. "You can have any shirt you like. In fact, have them all. I've got more on the *Firebrand*, and we can order clothing for you in any style or fabric you desire."

"That sounds nice, but I'd like some of my own clothes, too. Maybe I can get Gwen to bring me some of my clothes when she joins us." Lisa stretched up on her toes and kissed him. "C'mon, sexy. If we hurry, we can contact everyone and have time for a quickie in the shower before anyone gets here."

He scooped her into his arms and started jogging back to the ship, his heart light and a deep sense of contentment warming his soul. "You called me homeless the first night we met. At the time, I was insulted."

"And now?"

"Now I know where my home lies." He smiled down at her. "It's with you."

Lisa was sure her feet weren't touching the floor as she quickly donned another shirt and finger-combed the worst of the snarls and bits of grass out of her hair. Vadir's words had her walking on air, and every time he looked at her with those golden eyes, she floated a little higher.

Instead of the tiny communicator, Vadir activated a screen on a wall of his quarters and stood with his arm wrapped possessively around her waist as they waited for the *Firebrand* to respond.

"Where the Flames have you been? You've been untraceable for days!" The question roared out of the speaker before the visual component kicked in.

A second later, an image of a dark haired man with golden eyes and a scar slashed across one cheek appeared on the monitor. Everything about him, from his carefully trimmed hair and beard to the perfect symmetry of his posture, told her that this was a military man.

"Do you have to bellow like that?" Vadir demanded before turning to gesture to Lisa. "Commander Kash Denza, I'd like to introduce you to my mate, Lisa Woods. Lisa, the big male roaring like a wounded *brashi* is the commander of the *Firebrand* and the head of the prince's private guard. And to answer your question, my ship is currently in an impact crater on a mountain outside of the city. You couldn't locate us because we had to shunt what little power we had to life support and maintaining the shields to avoid human detection."

"Hi," Lisa waved at the monitor.

"Hello." The big man cracked a tiny smile. "I'm

pleased to know you're alive and well, Lisa. I have someone here who is going to be very happy to hear it."

"Is Maggie there already?" she asked.

Kash shook his head, but before he could answer Vadir leaned in closer to the screen. "By the Flames of the First One, you found your mate. How?"

She didn't know if it was wishful thinking or a flash of clairvoyant insight, but Lisa was sure she knew what had happened. "You're Gwen's mate!'

This time, Kash actually broke into a proud smile. "I am. May the Gods be blessed for their generosity."

Lisa squealed and bounced in place. "Where is she? Is she with you? Where's Maggie? They're all okay, aren't they? Holy shit, I can't believe it. I am totally taking credit for this. Signing up for Star-Crossed was all my idea and look how well this turned out!"

"Gwen is fine. She's resting at the moment, but I will wake her with the news that you've been located. She's been worried. Having both of her friends disappear on the same night…"

"I wish I could have let her know I was okay. Please tell her that, will you?"

"You can tell her yourself when we arrive in the shuttle." Kash turned his attention to Vadir again. "I take it the *Redshift* is not flight capable?"

"Not yet. Cas has managed most of the repairs, but I've got a short list of parts and supplies we'll need.

After that, it will be a matter of hours. Less if you and his royal highness are willing to get your hands dirty."

"Joran will help, or I'll kick his ass from here to Pyros. His parents want him home so that they can welcome his mate into the family and confirm his right of ascension. The sooner, the better was what the king told me. Our mates will not have long to say their goodbyes."

Lisa piped up. "Vee and I have figured out a way to get around the Council's stupid rule about first contact. If this works, we won't have to say goodbye, because we'll be able to come back."

"Is that so?"

Vadir's arm tightened around her waist. "It was Lisa who figured it out. I just need to find a way to sell it to the council."

Kash snorted. "You could sell a Romaki snow dragon its body weight in ice cubes. I have no doubt you'll manage."

"He's not that charming," Lisa chimed in. "If he was, we wouldn't have crashed."

Kash's eyebrow arched quizzically, but Vadir cut him off with a swipe of his hand.

"Don't ask. I'll explain when you and Joran are here, so I only have to tell the story once."

Chuckling, Kash nodded. "I can wait. Is there anything else you need me to bring?"

"Clothes. I need fresh clothes and a few things

from home. I don't suppose Gwen brought anything with her?" Lisa asked.

"Nothing that survived the Scorching," Kash replied with a trace of a blush on his cheeks.

He glanced away from the monitor, then turned back with a satisfied smile. "Joran is now in contact. He's with Maggie, and they are at your residence. I'll have him bring some things for you and Gwen and meet you at your coordinates."

"Perfect, thank you. And tell Gwen the cookies were the perfect energy food."

"I will tell her." Kash's eyes gleamed brighter for a second. "And I agree about the cookies."

After that, Vadir and Kash lapsed into Pyrosian, and a few minutes later the conversation ended.

The moment they were alone, she squealed with joy and threw her arms around Vee's neck, jumping up to wrap her arms around his hips. "This is great. Gwen and Maggie are fine, and we're going to Pyros together. Kash seems really nice. I can't believe he's Gwen's mate. I can't wait to meet Joran, too. This is going to be amazing."

Vadir laughed and walked over to the bed, his hands already busy removing the shirt she'd just donned. "Do you have any idea how beautiful you are when you are happy like this? You're glowing right now."

"I don't think I've ever been this happy. The only

one who has ever made me feel like this is you." She brushed her lips across his. "Do your people believe in love?"

He wrapped his arms around her and held her tight, his eyes staring into hers. "We believe that love grows from the slow-burning embers left after the Scorching has passed. I never expected to feel it, but now I do. I look forward to falling in love with you for the rest of my life."

Light and joy bubbled up inside her, overflowing her heart and making her soul sing. She opened the link between them, letting him feel all that was in her heart. She'd always dreamed of travelling the world and finding places to inspire her art. The Gods of Pyros had given her so much more. Instead of seeing just one world, she was going to travel amongst the stars with the man who would inspire her for the rest of her days.

THE END

KASH

Star-crossed Alien Mail Order Brides #3

What do you do when your planet runs out of women? Send for takeout, of course.

Kash knows he'll never be allowed to claim a mate. A lifetime of military service has left him too battle-scarred and broken to be considered for the off-world mating project his rulers have created to save their people.

His job is to make sure the more fortunate males get to Earth to retrieve their mates. All he has to do is pilot the ship, stay undetected, and keep an eye on things from orbit. It should be the easiest mission of his career...until he lays eyes on the one thing he never expected to find. His mate.

This book contains a hopeful romantic who is giving up hope and a soldier who is about to discover that love doesn't obey orders, and it can't be bound by rules.

Keep Reading for a peek at Kash and Gwen's story.

KASH - CHAPTER 1

"This was supposed to be an easy mission!" Kash muttered to himself as he drummed his fingers on the edge of the console that controlled his ship's systems. All he had to do was maintain orbit around Earth, keep the *Firebrand* off the humans' primitive tracking systems, and wait for his charges to acquire their mates and return to the ship. It should have been simple.

Simple had taken a steep dive into the heart of a star shortly after the mission started. Joran, heir to the throne of Pyros, Crown Prince, and a royal pain in the ass, had decided to leave his ship early, ditching his contingent of bodyguards along the way. The future king was currently wandering the city of Vancouver alone and unguarded because apparently, he couldn't tell the difference between the royal gardens of Pyros and the threat-infested streets of this primitive world.

He slapped a hand down on the console and opened a communication channel to one of prince's guards, audio only. They were on the planet below, looking for their missing charge.

"Yes, Commander Denza?" Guardsman Tarjen answered almost instantly.

"Tell me you've found him."

"No, sir. Not yet."

The drumming started again, faster this time. "Do you have any idea where he might have gone?"

"No, sir. He teleported out and programmed the system to erase the coordinates once he rematerialized. We're currently scanning for him, but it would appear he's switched off his locator."

"Where do you think he might be headed? It's not like he's ever been to Earth before. We're not even supposed to be in this part of the galaxy. His only reason for being here is to locate his mate. I suggest you start by figuring out where she is right now and ascertain if the prince is with her."

"Keth is already looking into that. We believe she is at her place of work, but we have been instructed not to approach her until contact has been made. Additionally, her workplace is in a heavy traffic area. There's nowhere nearby we can teleport without being seen."

That was one of the many problems with this *simple* mission. They didn't have permission to be here, and they were operating in total secrecy. The humans had no idea they were being visited by aliens, and it had to stay that way.

"Find the nearest safe location and make the rest of the journey on foot. I'm going to attempt to contact the prince again. If he doesn't respond soon, I'm going to come down there and kick his royal ass myself."

"Yes, sir!" Targen didn't bother to hide his amusement at Kash's statement.

They had all served together. Joran and his guards as fellow soldiers, and Kash as their commanding officer. Targen knew Kash meant every word of his threat. If the prince didn't report in soon, he'd be wearing Kash's boot-print on his ass.

He hit another button and opened a channel to his second charge, Vadir Rahal.

"Checking up on me, Commander?" Vadir owned and ran an intergalactic corporation. As one of the richest and most powerful men on the planet, he wasn't used to reporting to anyone. Not even for his own safety.

"That's more or less my entire job for this mission. What's your status?"

"My match has responded to the email, and I'm communicating with her now. Things are progressing. I have every reason to believe she will meet me for the evening meal at the designated location. Everything is going according to plan."

"That's good to hear. Do us all a favour and keep it that way."

Vadir chuckled. "Judging by your tone, I'd hazard a guess that Joran is already doing his own thing?"

"Something like that."

"This is why you should have taken me up on my offer to work for me instead of the royal family. I actually listen to the people I employ. Not to mention, I pay far better."

Kash snorted. "Ask me again after this mission is over. If anything happens to the prince, I'm going to be looking for a new job."

If he failed in this mission, he'd lose more than his job. He'd fought hard to be recognized on his own merits instead of relying on his family's influence. A lifetime of hard work, loyalty, and sacrifice had earned him his current rank. All of that was in jeopardy if this mission didn't go as planned.

"Joran can take care of himself, and so can I. Don't worry so much, Commander. We'll be back on board with our females before you know it. It's really a shame we can't initiate formal contact with this species. I could make a fortune just selling them environmental regulators and weather control satellites."

"Don't even think about it."

Vadir sighed. "I know. I know. Stick to the plan. I still haven't forgiven her Highness for doing this to me.

I don't have time for a mate right now. I've got deals to make and a business to run."

"Not even you can ignore a royal decree, Vadir. When the king commands us, we must obey."

Vadir signed off, then, and Kash was left alone with his thoughts. His fingers started drumming on the edge of the console as he wondered what he'd done to make the Gods hate him so much. Not that his life was one of hardship or despair. He had made his own way in the world, made his family proud, and had gained the the trust of the most powerful family on Pyros. But pride was a poor companion, and duty was no replacement for a mate and a family.

He'd accepted that there was no mate for him on Pyros. It was a realization that many males had faced. With seven males born for every female, the odds simply were not in his favour. But then, when the scouts had discovered that compatible matches existed elsewhere in the galaxy, he'd dared to hope again.

He should have known better.

Only young, fit males from important and influential families were even considered for potential matches with the human females. Logically, it made sense. Those families had the means to fund this endeavour, and the power to keep the attention of the Inter-Planetary Council focused elsewhere. Young, healthy men would make good fathers and be able to protect their mates and younglings. Logical or not, it had still been a bitter draught to swallow.

Even if the mission was successful and the matches were later opened to other males, he would never be considered. He was past his prime, and no female would want an aging, battle-scarred veteran when there were so many handsome young males to choose from.

The Gods had chosen another path for him, one of solitude, loyalty, and the honours that came with a life spent in service to the crown. It was enough. It would have to be. With no chance at a mate or a family, his career was the only legacy he had.

Gwen pulled the last batch of brownies out of the oven and then looked around the kitchen in dismay as she realized she was out of room. Every inch of countertop and her small kitchen table were already in use. She popped the brownies back into the oven and scrambled to transfer the chocolate chip cookies from their cooling trays to an old-fashioned cookie tin that had once been her grandmother's.

As she stacked the cookies in tiny towers inside the battered and dented tin, she recalled the countless times she'd done this with her Gran. Back then, baking had seemed like magic. Carefully combining ingredients, watching them come together in the ancient mixer, then the pouring of batter and the careful placement of each ball of dough so that none of the golden, crispy edges would touch when they were done.

When she was feeling down, Gwen baked. It was comforting. The familiar scents, the routine of it. If she closed her eyes, sometimes she could almost hear her Gran quietly humming and feel the old woman's warm, loving presence. It soothed her, and for a little while, the world would be a good and peaceful place again. Today, she needed that.

The rain pattered against the kitchen window, loud enough to make her glance up and wonder how her two friends were faring. Hopefully, wherever they were, their dates had them out of the weather and were treating them like queens. They deserved it.

When there was enough space cleared, she popped the lid onto the cookie tin and went back to the oven to rescue her brownies. Without thinking, she reached in and grabbed the glass pan with her bare hand.

"Shit! Ow, shit, dammit." She yelped in pain, dropped the brownies, and dashed to the sink to run cold water over her burn.

"Good job, idiot." She scolded herself as she waited for the stream of cold water to ease the sting. It was a clear sign from the universe that it was time for her to stop baking and go to bed. She should have stopped hours ago. In fact, she had...for a little while. Lisa had come home from work and found her baking up a storm. Like the dear friend she was, she'd done what she could to cajole Gwen out of her dark mood. The levity had only lasted as long as Lisa's presence, though. When Lisa had headed out to meet her mystery date, Gwen had falling back into her funk.

Still holding her hand under the tap, she selected one of the still-warm cookies from its rack and munched on it while surveying the damage. The floor was strewn with chunks of brownie, and the glass pan was sitting upside-down with a massive crack showing across the bottom. She'd have to toss the whole mess out.

She started to cry, hot tears scalding her face as she looked at the mess on her floor. The ruined pan might as well have been named Gwen. She was as old and broken as it was, and she was being tossed aside, too. Her boss had given her the news today. The second-hand bookstore she'd worked at for years was closing down. The books she loved would be sold off, and the job she'd held for ten years would be gone.

On top of that, the same dating service that had provided her two best friends with their dates for the night had sent her a rejection email. She hadn't wanted to sign up in the first place, but Lisa had insisted, and between the wine and the ice cream, Gwen had given in. The Star-Crossed dating service specifically said it was for young women, though, and at thirty-five, she'd worried that she wouldn't make the cut.

Sure enough, at the same time her friends were being matched with drop-dead gorgeous guys, she'd been sent a politely worded letter informing her that she wasn't a match for anyone in their database, which was geared toward a younger age bracket. It was official. Just like the glass pan, her best days were behind her.

Maybe she should have agreed to go out with Shane, a customer who had been hanging out at the bookstore for months while he was 'between jobs.' He never bought anything, he just thumbed through the books, one hand in the pocket of his faded, too-tight shorts that puckered across the front and left nothing to the imagination.

He kept asking her to have a beer with him, but she'd always declined. Maybe it was time to stop fooling herself. Maybe Shane, with his nicotine-stained fingers and his awkward ways, was the best she could hope for.

How the hell had her life come to this? She'd always dreamed of having a family someday. Of sharing her life with someone who thought she was beautiful despite her curves. Yet, here she was, standing in her kitchen eating cookies alone on a Friday night with nothing to show for her life but an almost empty bank account and a job that was about to disappear.

She let herself wallow in self pity for three more cookies and then she made herself stop. Eating her feelings and moping wouldn't change a damned thing. All that would happen was she'd wind up feeling guilty about eating too much, and the cycle would begin again.

She dried her hand and carefully checked her fingers. Thankfully, there wasn't any real damage. Just a pair of small blisters that would only take a few days to heal. The way her day had gone, she could have wound up sitting in an emergency waiting room for hours.

"Ice and aloe, a baker's best friends." She broke off a piece of aloe from the plant on her windowsill, treated the burns with it, and then went to work cleaning up the mess on the floor. It wasn't easy to do one-handed, but she managed.

It was late by the time she finished cleaning up. The sugar rush from the cookies and brownies she'd nibbled on had faded away, leaving her tired and emotionally drained. She tossed the thawed-out ice pack back into the freezer and picked up her phone to check the time. Almost eleven, and no word from either Maggie or Lisa.

Unease and worry slithered into her chest and coiled around her heart. They should have checked in by now. The three of them set up a system years ago. Whenever one of them went out on a date, they'd check in to let the others know they were okay. Once when they arrived, and again when they were heading home. If things were going really well, they'd text or call and update on where they were heading next, and if they'd be out for the night.

Things were clearly going well for both her friends or they'd have sent a message by now. Should she act like a mother hen and call them for an update? She rejected that idea right away. Calling would be intrusive. She could text, though. She fired off a quick message to them both and hoped they wouldn't think she was overreacting. She just wanted to know they were safe before she tried to get some sleep.

Kash paced the floor of his quarters, too agitated to sleep. The prince had been located and was safely back on his private shuttle with his newly-acquired mate. That was the only thing that had gone right since Joran and Vadir had arrived on the planet. Both males were in the thrall of the Scorching, the mating fever that affected every Pyrosian when they first met their true mate. It shouldn't have been possible. Their matches weren't even the same species, but it *had* happened, twice.

That wasn't the end of the surprises, either. The prince had informed him that his mate did not live alone. She had not one but two friends who would notice her absence. How had that detail been missed? Their presence here was a secret, and they were breaking more than a few laws being in this part of the galaxy at all. First contact with a race as early in their development as the humans was completely forbidden. Because of that, the human females selected as matches were supposed to be unattached and easily removed without causing suspicion.

He smacked a hand against the hull. "We make plans while the Gods laugh."

It would be approximately two solar cycles before the newly mated pairs would be free of the effects of the Scorching. There was no way either female would be returning home until then. He needed to keep an eye on both residences and make sure that no one noticed Lisa or Maggie's absence. If they did—. Flames, what was he going to do if that happened? He couldn't do much from up here, and his orders required him to stay in orbit, overseeing everything. He wasn't supposed to get involved unless things were dire.

If the Gods were feeling generous, then the rest of the mission would go smoothly, and nothing else would go wrong. Something told him that wasn't going to be the case.

"Computer. Prepare two micro-drones for surveillance on the planet's surface. Urban setting. Maximum stealth mode."

"Confirmed. Destination?"

"Two different destinations. Target the home addresses on file for the human females matched to Vadir Rahal and Joran Pyros. Monitor and record any activity at both locations."

There was an unusually long pause before the ships AI spoke again. "Please reconfirm destinations. Data is in conflict with command given."

"Identify error."

"Home addresses on file differ, but coordinates do not."

"Details, computer. Give me the damned details."

"There is a minor variation between the two addresses, but both residences exist in the same structure."

He ran a hand through his hair and resisted the urge to try and punch a hole in the hull. "They live together? You're telling me that out of an entire city, the database managed to match two females who know each other?"

"I cannot confirm their social bonds based on current data, but statistically it seems likely the two females are acquainted, Commander."

"Display the two addresses side by side on wall

monitor one, then display all data collected on the females in that building on wall monitor two."

It didn't take long for him to see the problem. The address was numeric, but the last character was a letter, instead: 1665-A and 1665-C.

The Spark. The Scorching. And now the revelation that Joran and Vadir's mates were already acquainted. The Gods were in fine form today.

"I don't get paid enough for this. I swear after this mission is over I going to seriously consider working for Vadir," he muttered as he turned to look over the data now displayed on the second monitor.

"Computer, why are there three names being displayed? I asked you to show me the information on Vadir and Joran's matches."

"The Commander is incorrect. You asked me to display information on all the residents of that building."

A headache blossomed behind his eyes, adding to his misery. "Where did you get the information on the third female?"

"The Star-Crossed database included her information. Gwen Hudson was rejected as a potential match, but her information is still on file."

There were three of them. And the third one knew all about the Star-Crossed dating service. She would have to be dealt with before the others were transported to Pyros.

"Show me her file. Pictures. Data, all of it."

Information filled the monitor, but Kash didn't see it. All his attention was on the image the computer had placed at the top of the screen. A goddess stared back at him. Why was this beautiful, dark-skinned, lushly curved female dropped from the program?

He hadn't realized he'd spoken aloud until the computer responded to his question. "The female was determined to be past the prime breeding age for humans."

She was too old? He stared at her picture, unable to see any sign of infirmity or age. Her jet-black hair fell in tight spirals around her smiling face, and her skin was a warm, deep shade of brown that he'd never seen before. She was breathtaking. If she was an example of the females that were being rejected from the matching program, then the ones responsible were doing a great disservice to the males of his world.

"Send the drones to target location. Have one patrol the perimeter and have the second one enter the building and record all activity. If the inhabitant shows signs of becoming concerned or agitated, alert me immediately." He wasn't holding out much hope that the beauty on the planet below had no connection to the females already claimed by their Pyrosian mates, but he wouldn't take action until he had to. If the three were friends, it wouldn't be long before Gwen Hudson started to worry. When that happened, he'd have to do something, likely something that went against his orders.

Hopefully, by then, he'd have some idea what that would be because nothing in their mission plan covered this contingency. He was going to have to make things up as he went along.

He drummed his fingers against his thigh as he stared at Gwen's image on the monitor.

So much for simple.

ABOUT THE INTERGALACTIC DATING AGENCY SERIES

Ready for more out of this world romances? The adventure isn't over yet! Fly over to our dating agency website to check out more stories from this multi-author series. The Intergalactic Dating Agency is ready and waiting to set you up with a host of alien hotties from all over the galaxy.

Make a date with your alien match today.
http://romancingthealien.com

Or join the conversation in our Facebook Group
http://smarturl.it/RomancingTheAlien

ABOUT THE AUTHOR

Susan lives out on the Canadian west coast surrounded by open water, dear family, and good friends. She's jumped out of perfectly good airplanes on purpose and accidentally swum with sharks on the Great Barrier Reef.

If the world ends, she plans to survive as the spunky, comedic sidekick to the heroes of the new world, because she's too damned short and out of shape to make it on her own for long.

You can find out more about Susan and her books here:

www.susanhayes.ca

www.ingramcontent.com/pod-product-compliance
Lightning Source LLC
Chambersburg PA
CBHW021730190726
48288CB00009B/2981